Lil' Hellions

Created and Written by
Dwight L. MacPherson

Art and Letters by
Mathieu Benoit

Colors by
Mike Dolce & Jared Cole

Edited by
Lauren Perry

Production Assistance by
Thomas Mauer

ARCANA
www.arcana.com

CEO and Owner
Sean O'Reilly

VP of Operations
Mark Poulton

VP of Marketing
Tyler Nicol

VP of Special Projects
Nick Schley

Senior Editor
Mike Kalvoda

General Manager
Michelle Meyers

ISBN: 978-1-926914-37-4 Printed in Canada

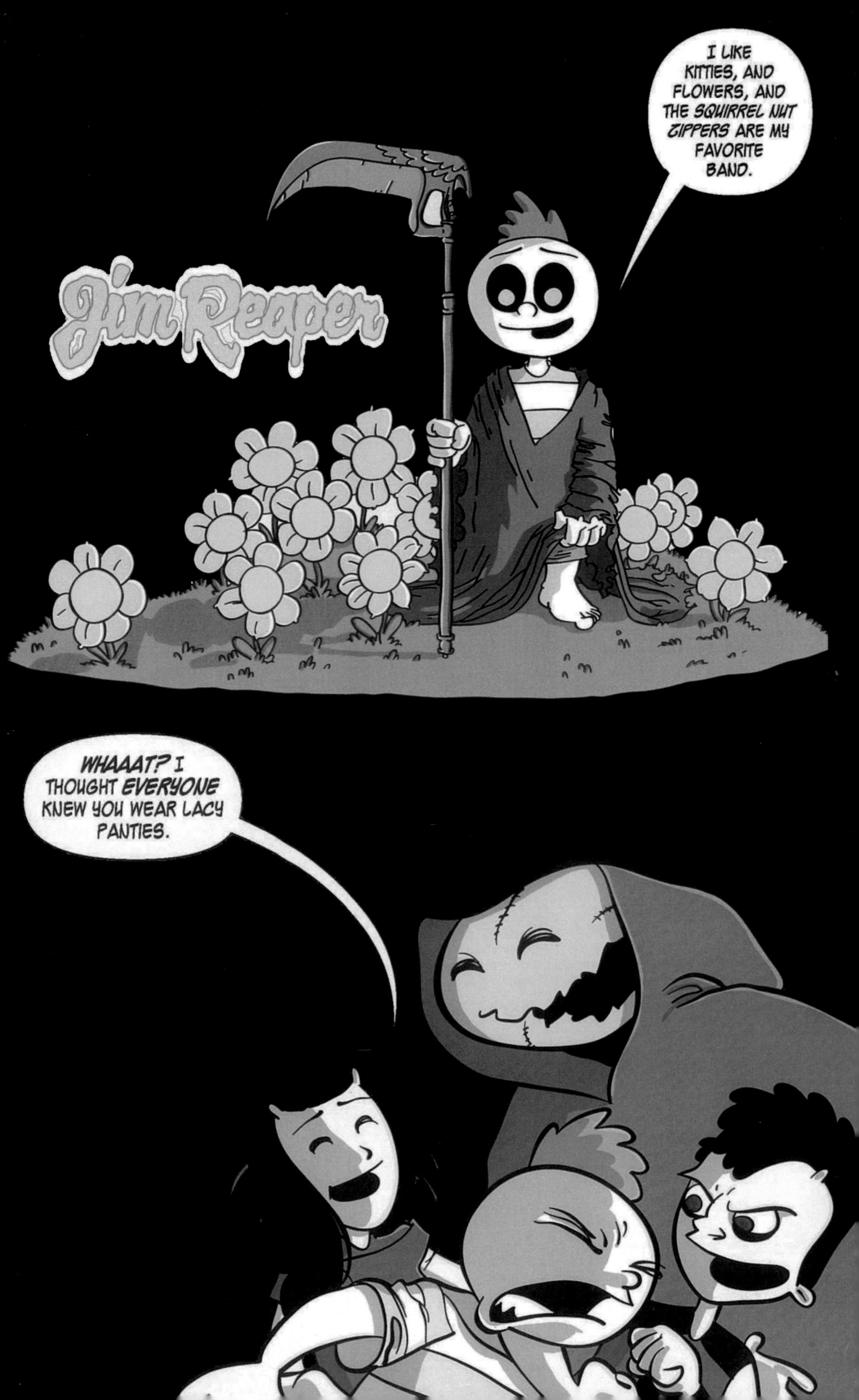
Jim Reaper
I LIKE KITTIES, AND FLOWERS, AND THE SQUIRREL NUT ZIPPERS ARE MY FAVORITE BAND.
WHAAAT? I THOUGHT EVERYONE KNEW YOU WEAR LACY PANTIES.

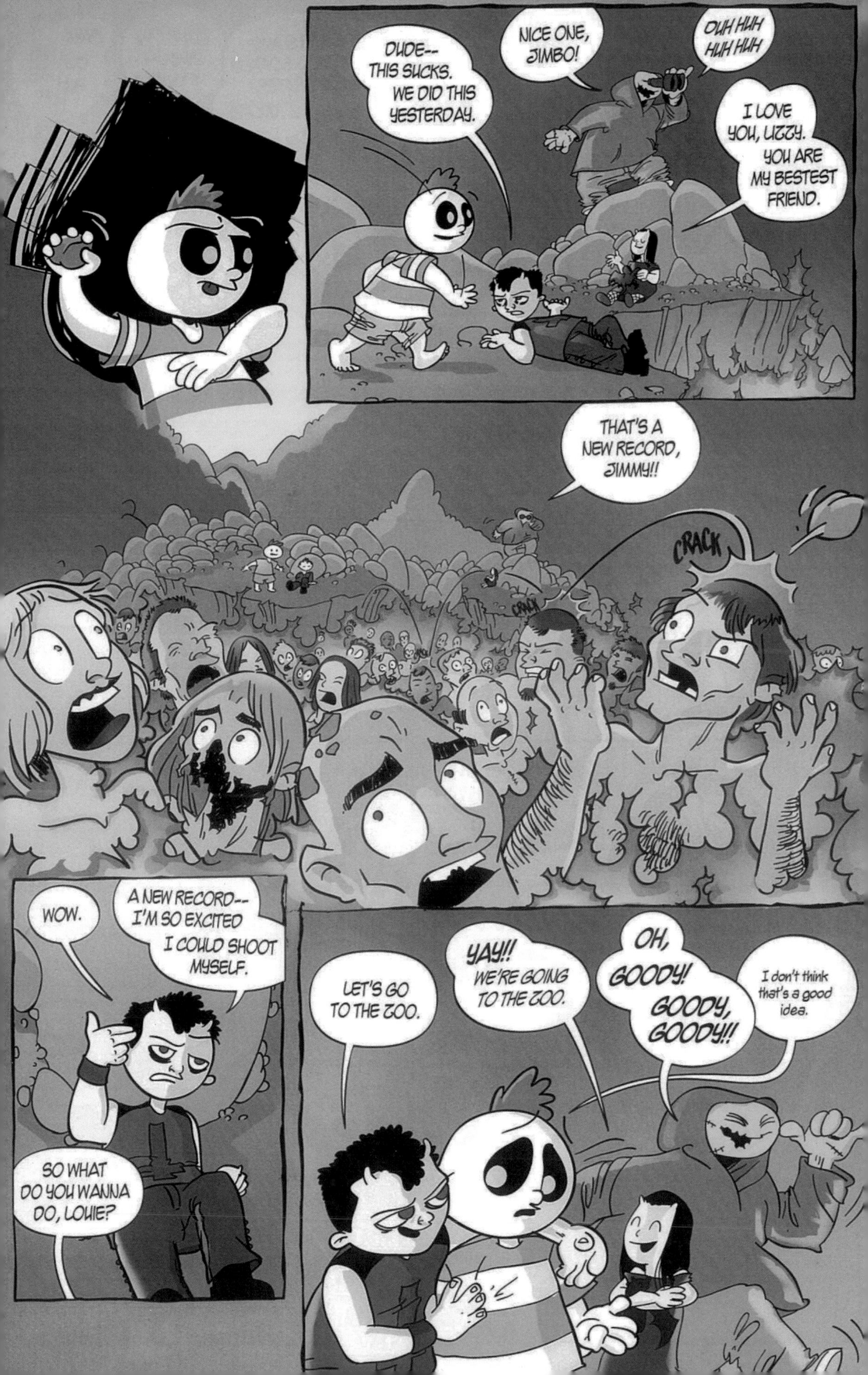
DUDE-- THIS SUCKS. WE DID THIS YESTERDAY.
NICE ONE, JIMBO!
OUH HUH HUH HUH
I LOVE YOU, UZZY. YOU ARE MY BESTEST FRIEND.
THAT'S A NEW RECORD, JIMMY!!
CRACK
CRACK
WOW.
A NEW RECORD-- I'M SO EXCITED I COULD SHOOT MYSELF.
SO WHAT DO YOU WANNA DO, LOUIE?
LET'S GO TO THE ZOO.
YAY!! WE'RE GOING TO THE ZOO.
OH, GOODY! GOODY, GOODY!!
I don't think that's a good idea.

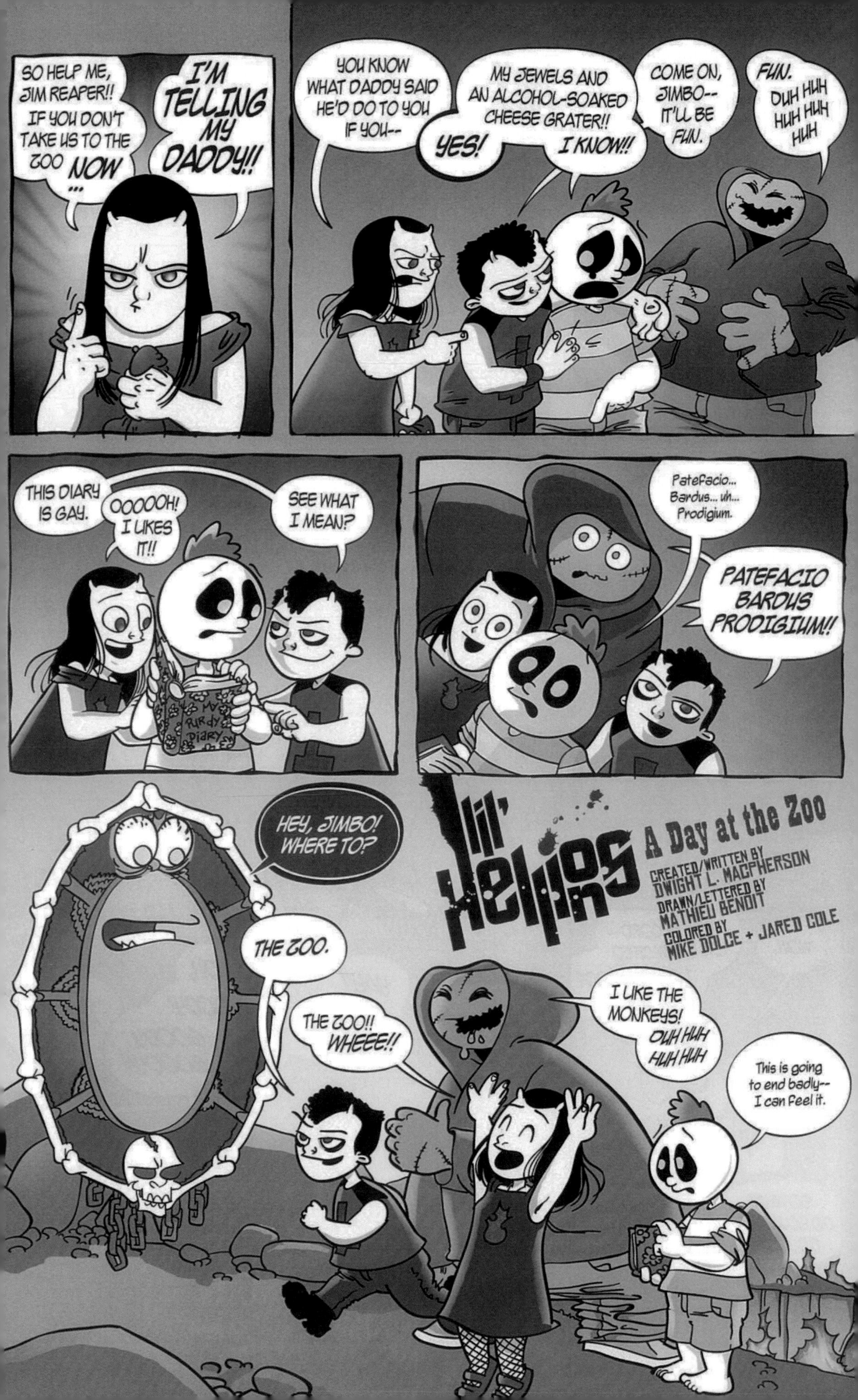
SO HELP ME, JIM REAPER!! IF YOU DON'T TAKE US TO THE ZOO NOW ...
I'M TELLING MY DADDY!!
YOU KNOW WHAT DADDY SAID HE'D DO TO YOU IF YOU--
YES!
MY JEWELS AND AN ALCOHOL-SOAKED CHEESE GRATER!!
I KNOW!!
COME ON, JIMBO-- IT'LL BE FUN.
FUN. OUH HUH HUH HUH HUH
THIS DIARY IS GAY.
OOOOOH! I LIKES IT!!
SEE WHAT I MEAN?
MY PURDY DIARY
Patefacio... Bardus... uh... Prodigium.
PATEFACIO BARDUS PRODIGIUM!!
HEY, JIMBO! WHERE TO?
THE ZOO.
Lil' Hellions
A Day at the Zoo
CREATED/WRITTEN BY DWIGHT L. MACPHERSON
DRAWN/LETTERED BY MATHIEU BENOIT
COLORED BY MIKE DOLCE + JARED COLE
THE ZOO!! WHEEE!!
I LIKE THE MONKEYS! OUH HUH HUH HUH
This is going to end badly-- I can feel it.

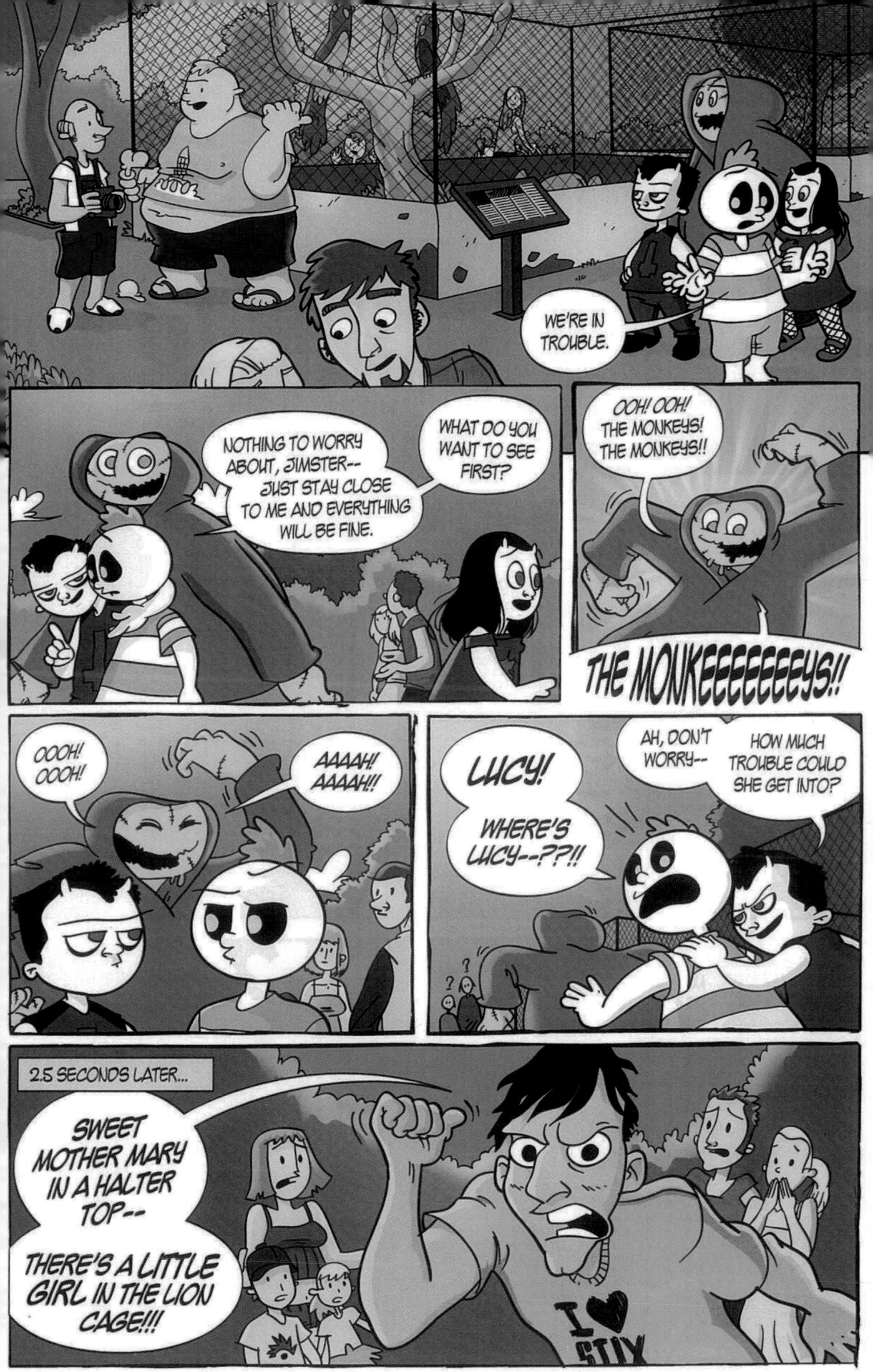
WE'RE IN TROUBLE.
NOTHING TO WORRY ABOUT, JIMSTER-- JUST STAY CLOSE TO ME AND EVERYTHING WILL BE FINE.
WHAT DO YOU WANT TO SEE FIRST?
OOH! OOH! THE MONKEYS! THE MONKEYS!!
THE MONKEEEEEEEEYS!!
OOOH! OOOH!
AAAAH! AAAAH!!
LUCY!
WHERE'S LUCY--??!!
AH, DON'T WORRY--
HOW MUCH TROUBLE COULD SHE GET INTO?
2.5 SECONDS LATER...
SWEET MOTHER MARY IN A HALTER TOP--
THERE'S A LITTLE GIRL IN THE LION CAGE!!!
I ♥ STIX

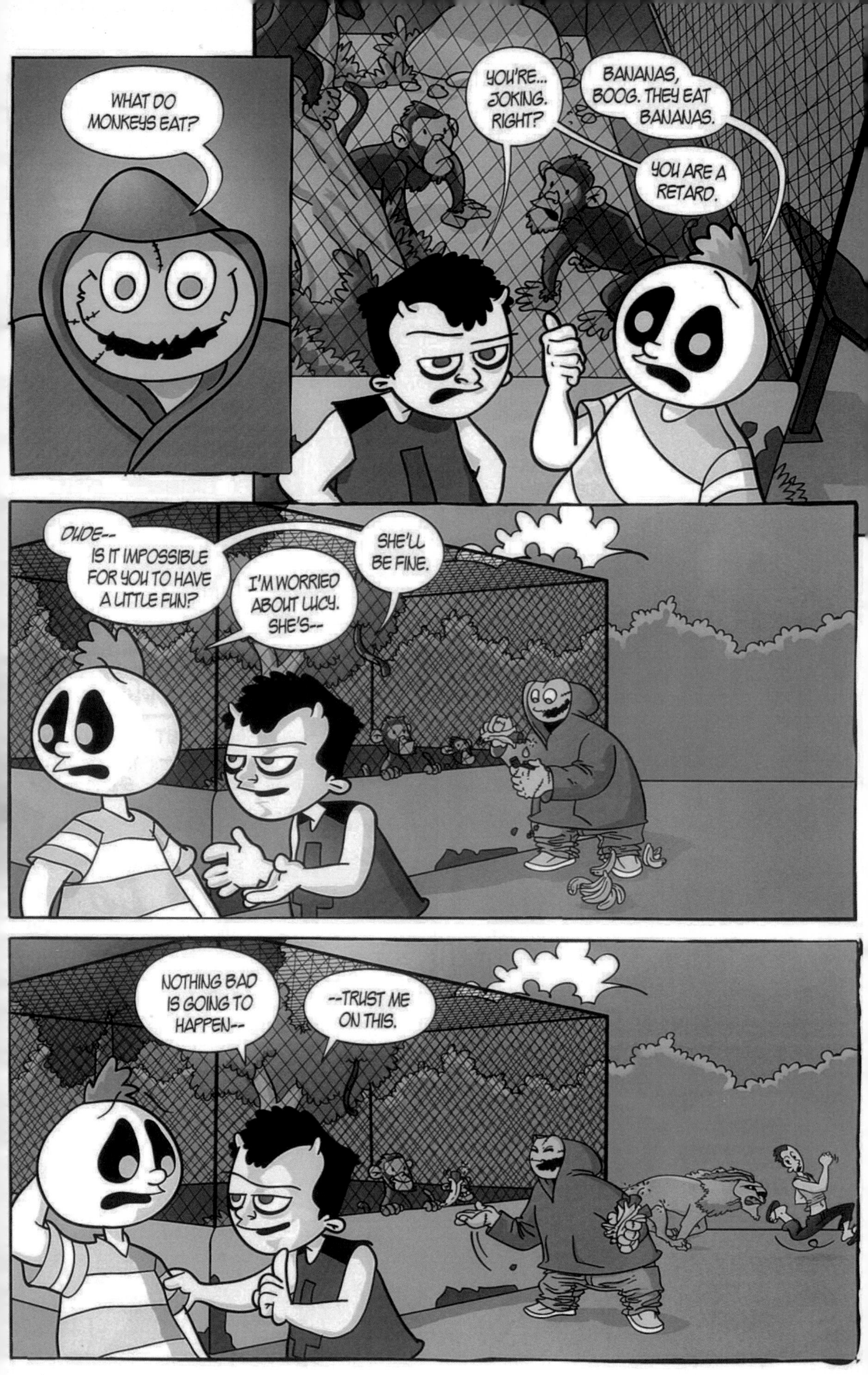
WHAT DO MONKEYS EAT?
YOU'RE... JOKING. RIGHT?
BANANAS, BOOG. THEY EAT BANANAS.
YOU ARE A RETARD.
DUDE-- IS IT IMPOSSIBLE FOR YOU TO HAVE A LITTLE FUN?
I'M WORRIED ABOUT LUCY. SHE'S--
SHE'LL BE FINE.
NOTHING BAD IS GOING TO HAPPEN--
--TRUST ME ON THIS.

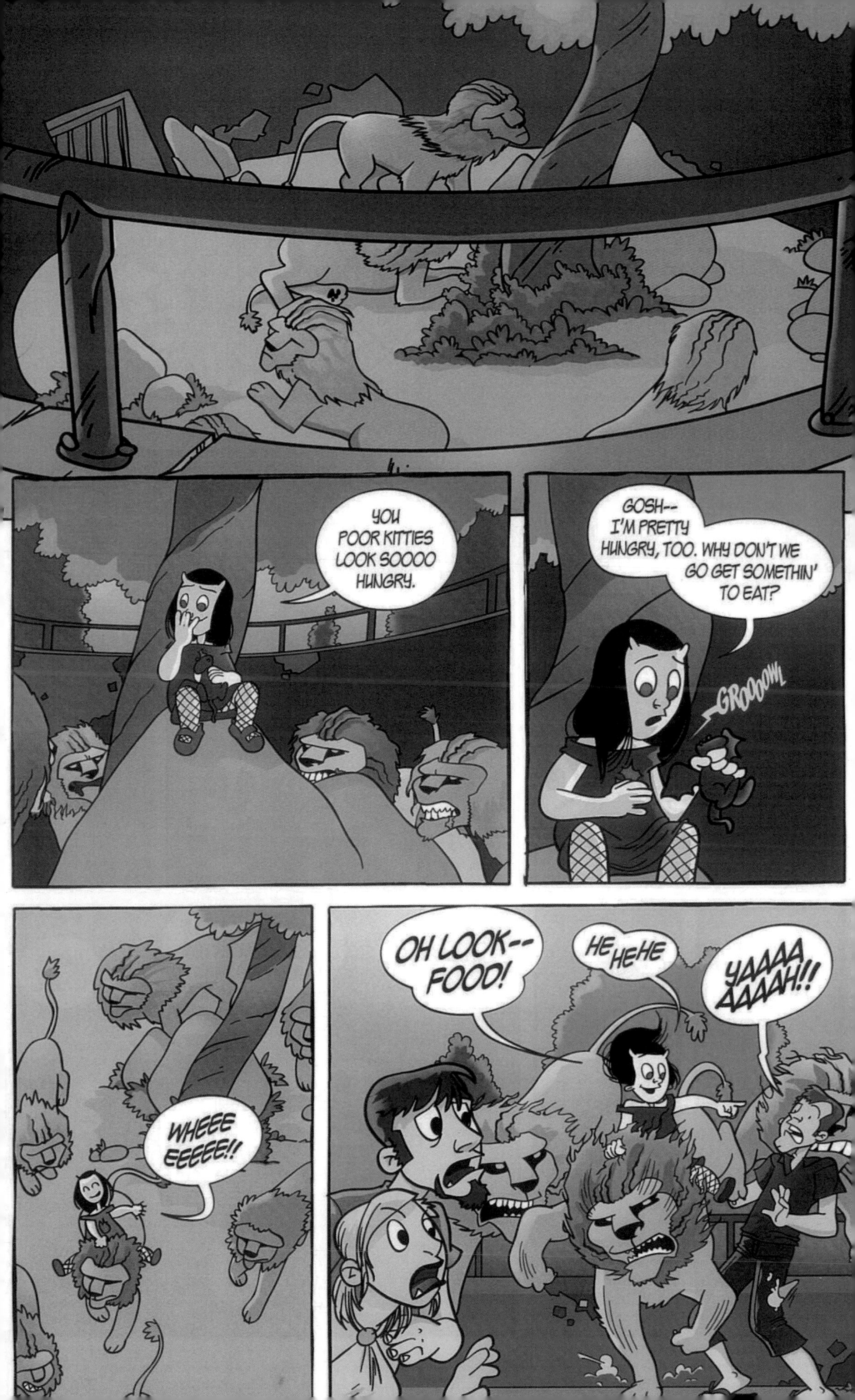
YOU POOR KITTIES LOOK SOOOO HUNGRY.
GOSH-- I'M PRETTY HUNGRY, TOO. WHY DON'T WE GO GET SOMETHIN' TO EAT?
GROOOOWL
WHEEE EEEEE!!
OH LOOK-- FOOD!
HE HEHE
YAAAA AAAAH!!

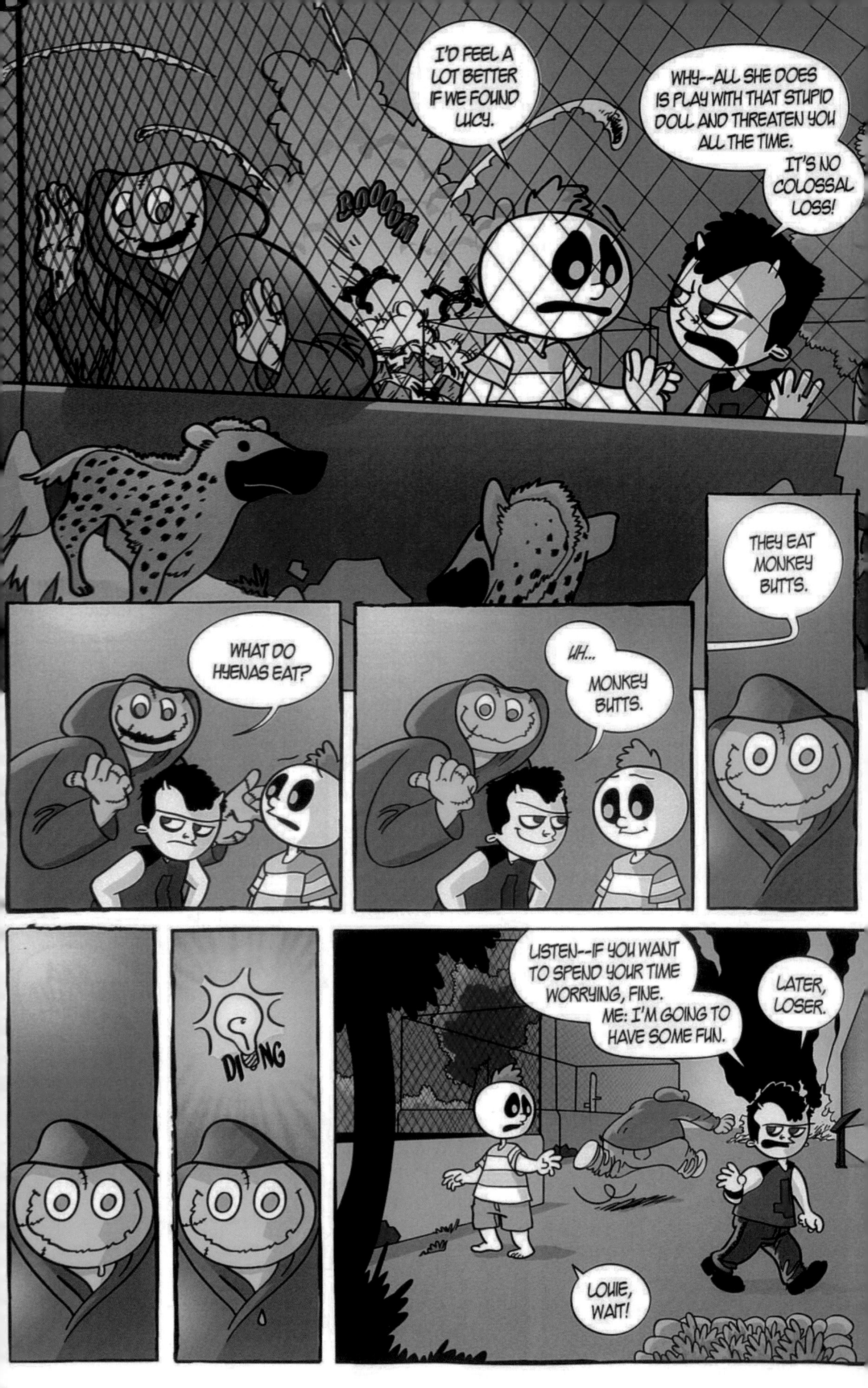
I'D FEEL A LOT BETTER IF WE FOUND LUCY.
WHY--ALL SHE DOES IS PLAY WITH THAT STUPID DOLL AND THREATEN YOU ALL THE TIME.
IT'S NO COLOSSAL LOSS!
WHAT DO HYENAS EAT?
UH...
MONKEY BUTTS.
THEY EAT MONKEY BUTTS.
DING
LISTEN--IF YOU WANT TO SPEND YOUR TIME WORRYING, FINE.
ME: I'M GOING TO HAVE SOME FUN.
LATER, LOSER.
LOUIE, WAIT!

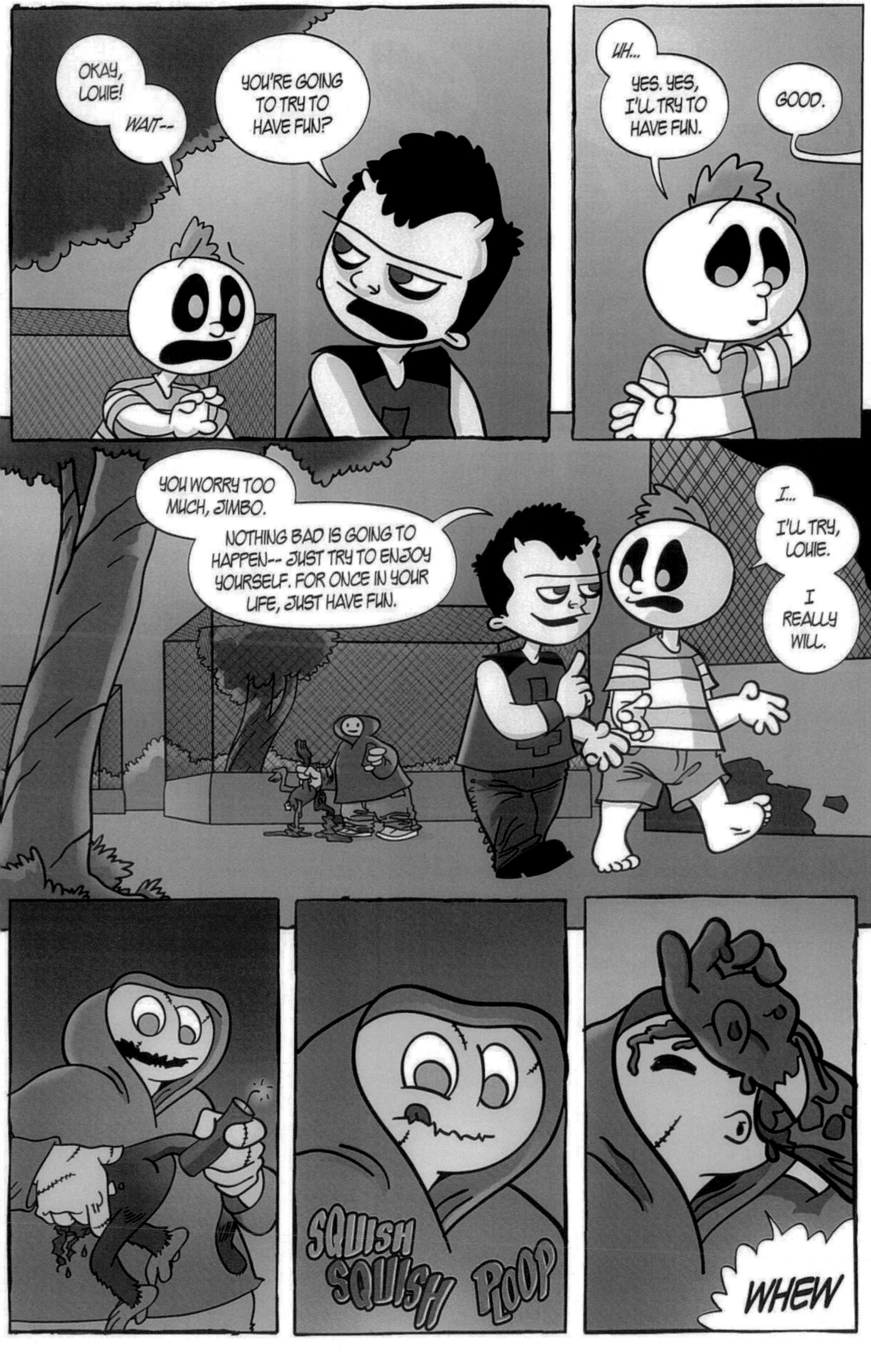
OKAY, LOUIE!
WAIT--
YOU'RE GOING TO TRY TO HAVE FUN?
UH...
YES. YES, I'LL TRY TO HAVE FUN.
GOOD.
YOU WORRY TOO MUCH, JIMBO.
NOTHING BAD IS GOING TO HAPPEN-- JUST TRY TO ENJOY YOURSELF. FOR ONCE IN YOUR LIFE, JUST HAVE FUN.
I...
I'LL TRY, LOUIE.
I REALLY WILL.
SQUISH
SQUISH
PLOOP
WHEW

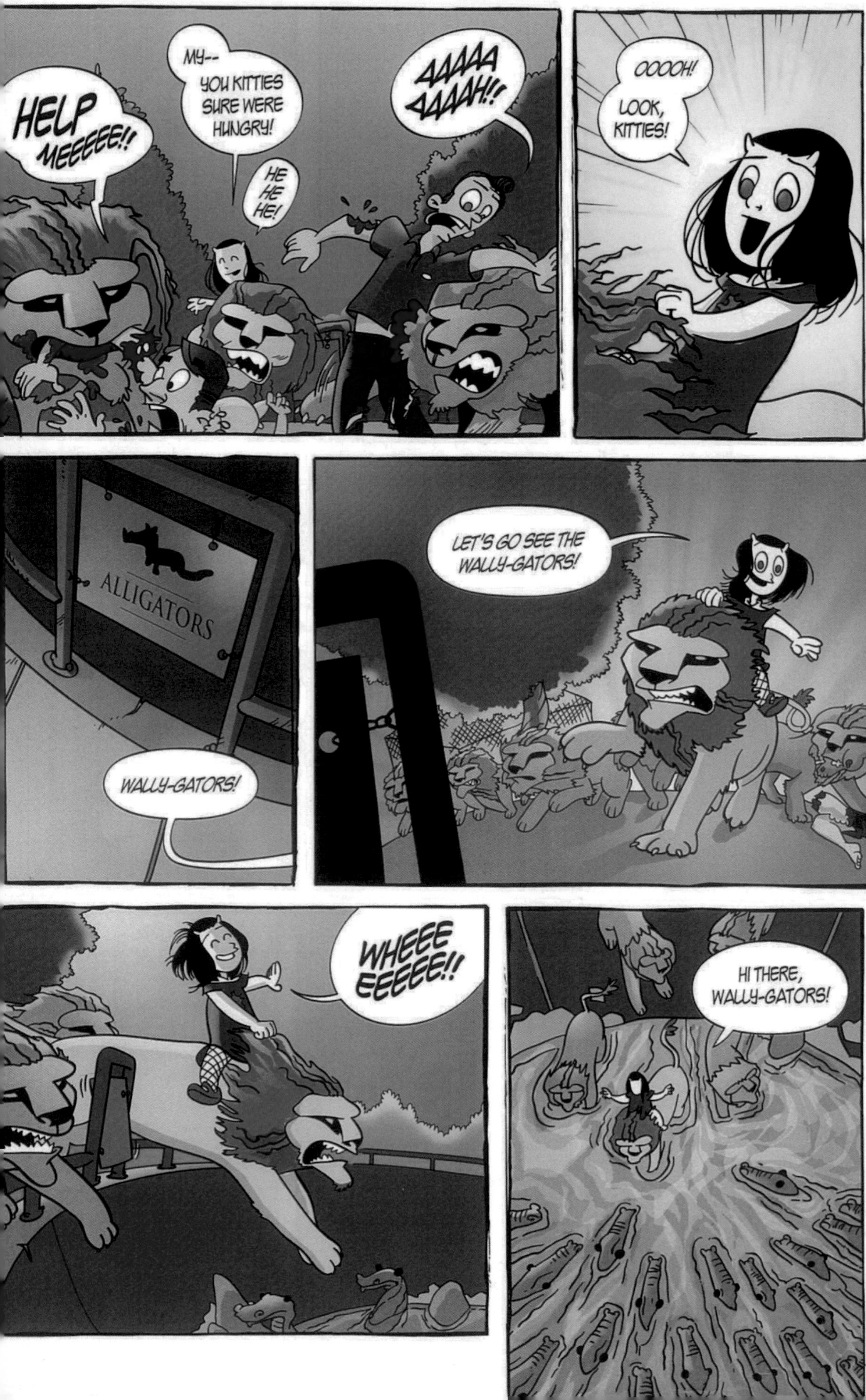
HELP MEEEEE!!
MY-- YOU KITTIES SURE WERE HUNGRY!
HE HE HE!
AAAAA AAAAH!!
OOOOH!
LOOK, KITTIES!
ALLIGATORS
WALLY-GATORS!
LET'S GO SEE THE WALLY-GATORS!
WHEEE EEEEE!!
HI THERE, WALLY-GATORS!

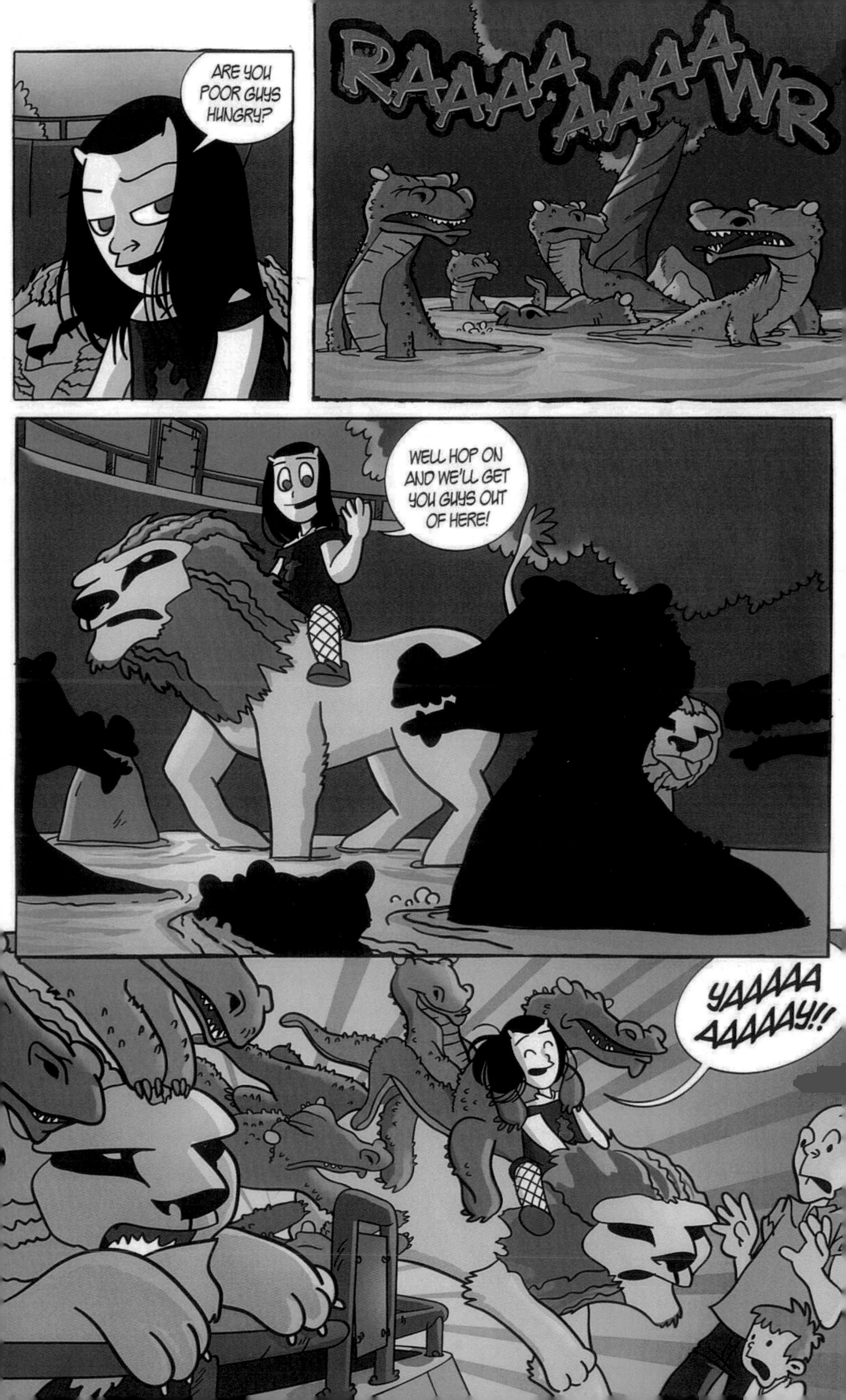
ARE YOU POOR GUYS HUNGRY?
RAAAAAAAAWR
WELL HOP ON AND WE'LL GET YOU GUYS OUT OF HERE!
YAAAAAAAAAY!!

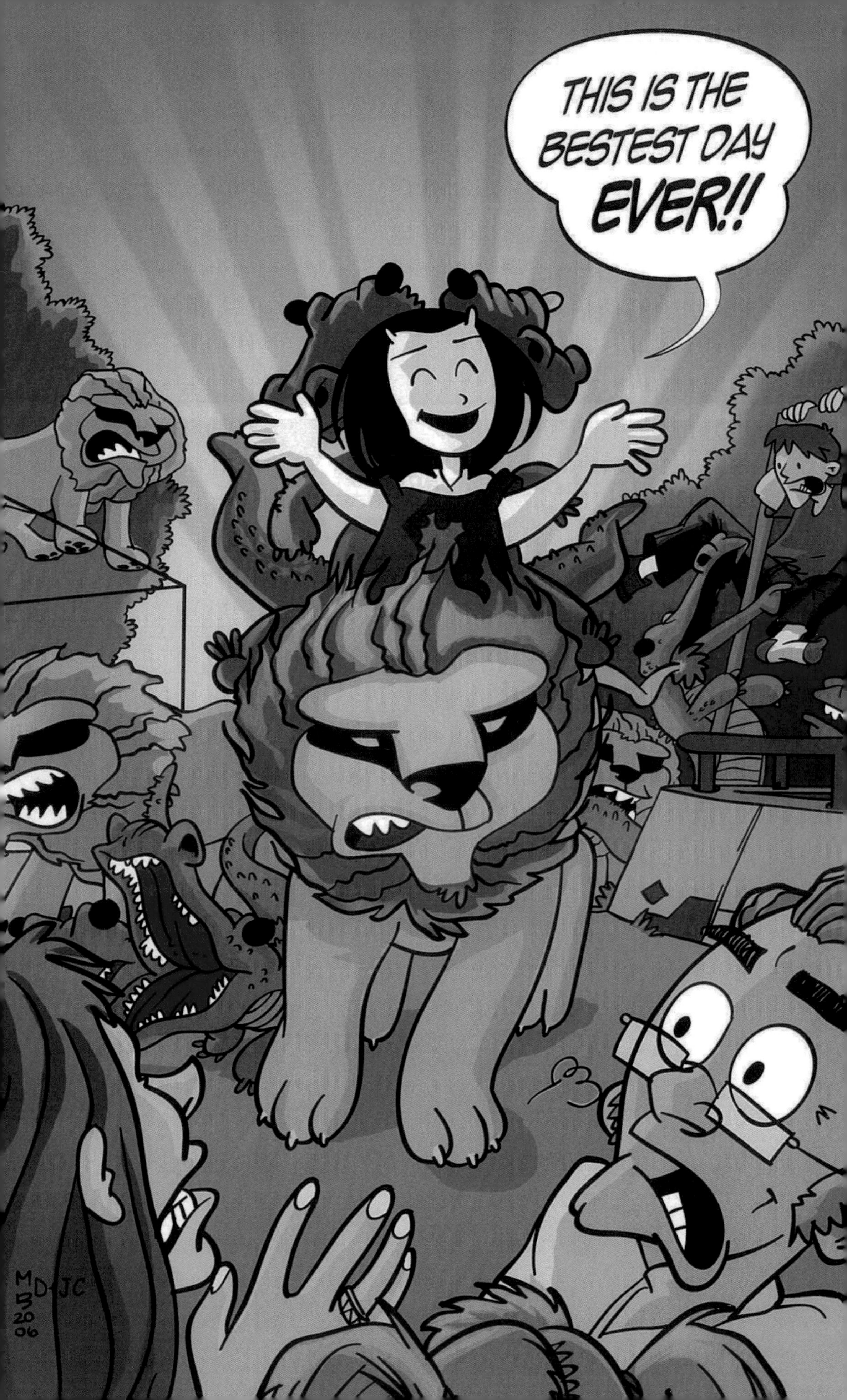
THIS IS THE BESTEST DAY EVER!!
MD·JC MB 2006

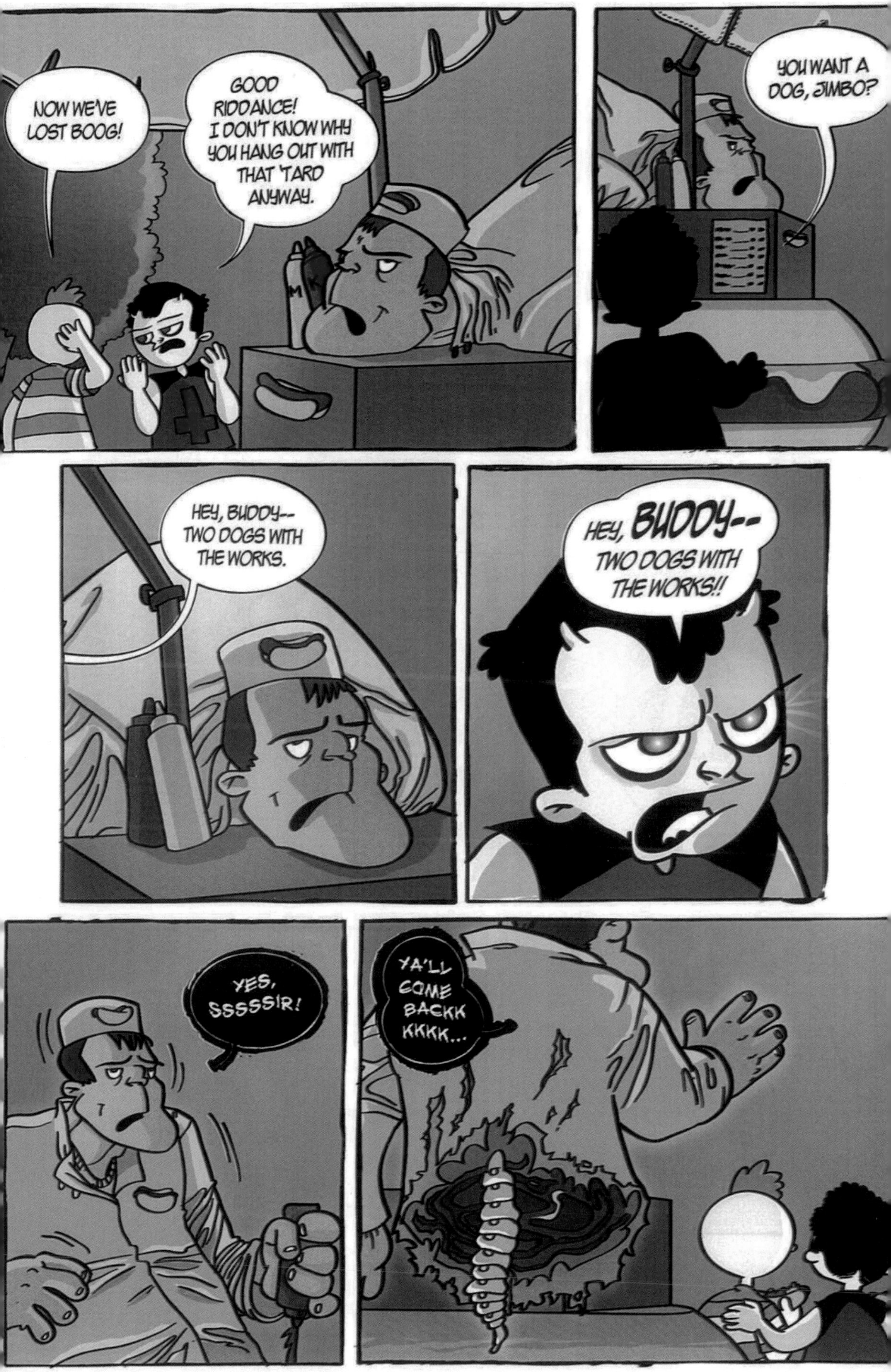
NOW WE'VE LOST BOOG!
GOOD RIDDANCE! I DON'T KNOW WHY YOU HANG OUT WITH THAT 'TARD ANYWAY.
YOU WANT A DOG, JIMBO?
HEY, BUDDY-- TWO DOGS WITH THE WORKS.
HEY, BUDDY-- TWO DOGS WITH THE WORKS!!
YES, SSSSSIR!
YA'LL COME BACKK KKKK...

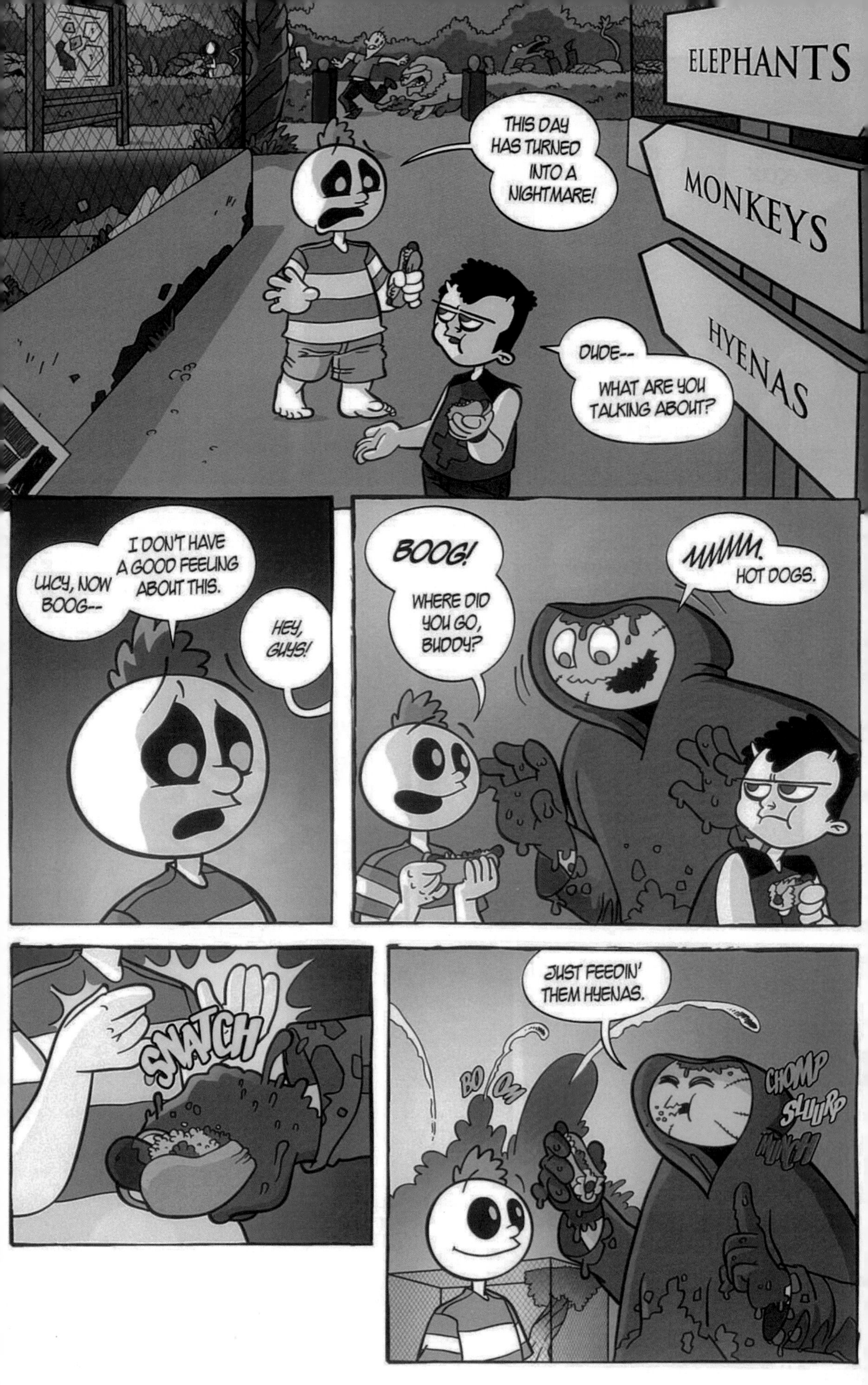
ELEPHANTS
MONKEYS
HYENAS
THIS DAY HAS TURNED INTO A NIGHTMARE!
DUDE-- WHAT ARE YOU TALKING ABOUT?
LUCY, NOW BOOG--
I DON'T HAVE A GOOD FEELING ABOUT THIS.
HEY, GUYS!
BOOG!
WHERE DID YOU GO, BUDDY?
MMMM. HOT DOGS.
SNATCH
JUST FEEDIN' THEM HYENAS.
BOOM
CHOMP
SLUURP
MUNCH

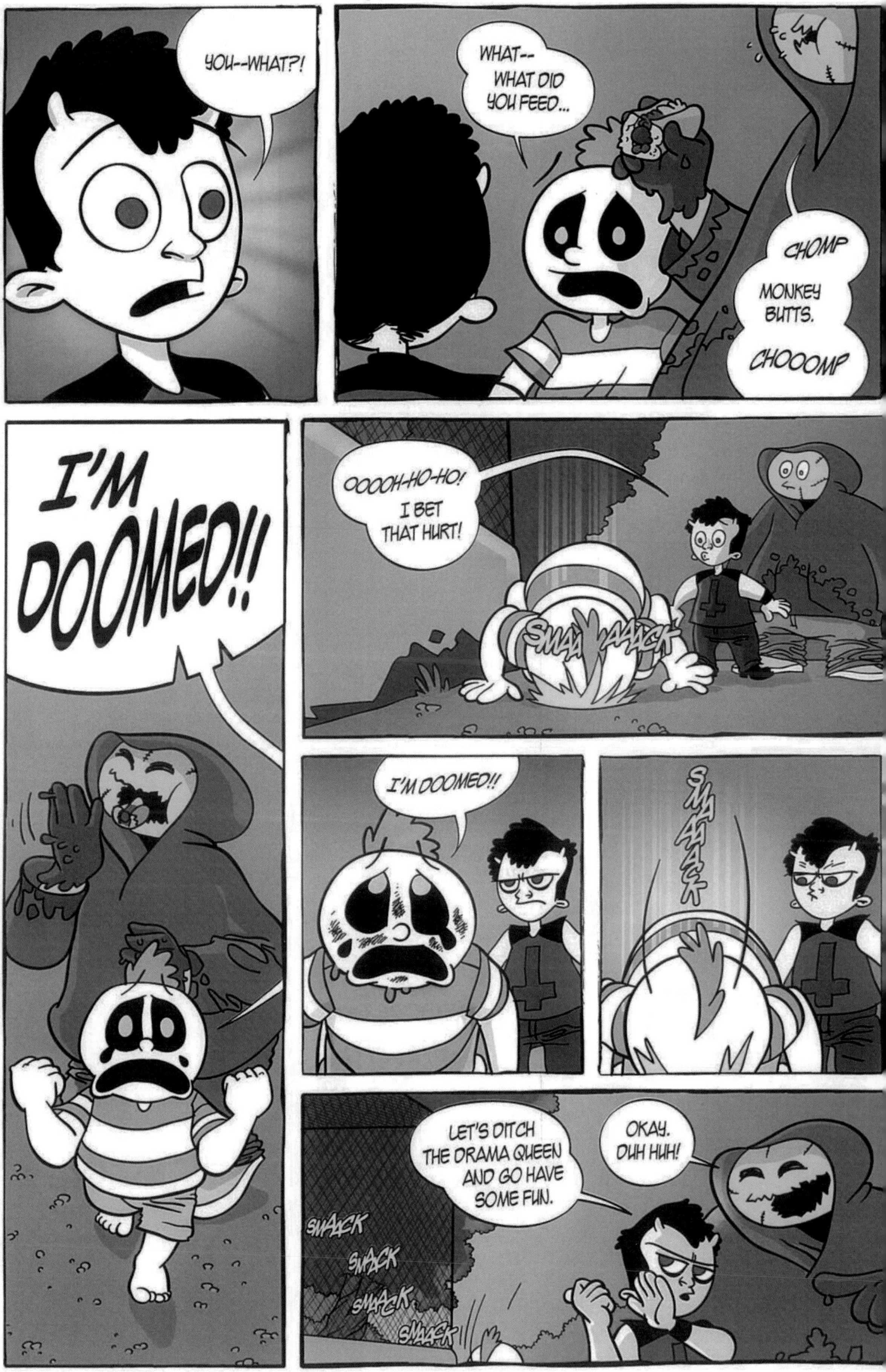
YOU--WHAT?!
WHAT-- WHAT DID YOU FEED...
CHOMP
MONKEY BUTTS.
CHOOOMP
I'M DOOMED!!
OOOOH-HO-HO! I BET THAT HURT!
SMAAAAAACK
I'M DOOMED!!
SMAAAACK
LET'S DITCH THE DRAMA QUEEN AND GO HAVE SOME FUN.
OKAY. DUH HUH!
SMAACK
SMACK
SMAACK
SMAACK

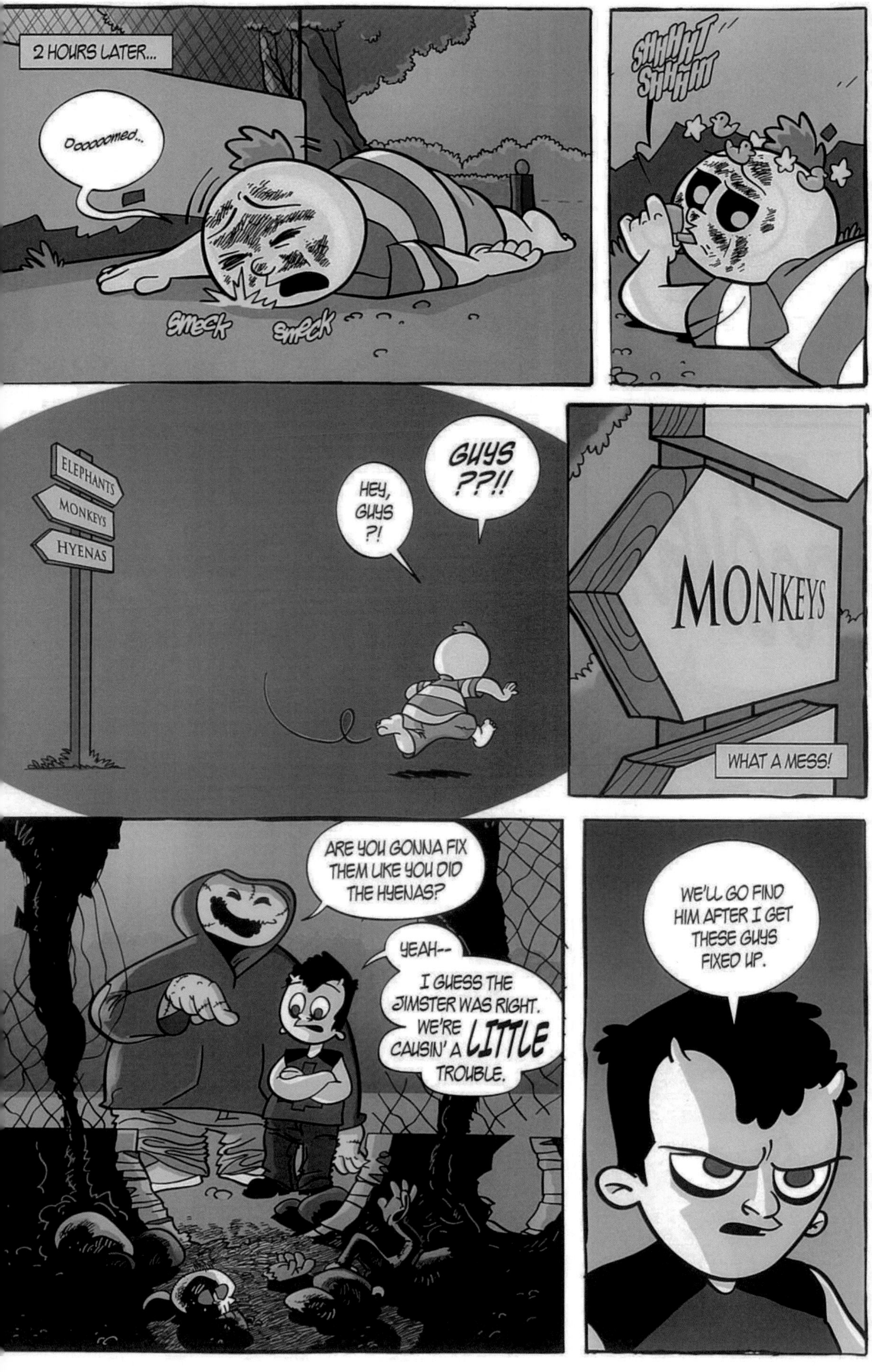
2 HOURS LATER...
Oooooomed...
SMECK
SMECK
SHHHHT SHHHHT
HEY, GUYS ?!
GUYS ??!!
ELEPHANTS
MONKEYS
HYENAS
MONKEYS
WHAT A MESS!
ARE YOU GONNA FIX THEM LIKE YOU DID THE HYENAS?
YEAH--
I GUESS THE JIMSTER WAS RIGHT. WE'RE CAUSIN' A LITTLE TROUBLE.
WE'LL GO FIND HIM AFTER I GET THESE GUYS FIXED UP.

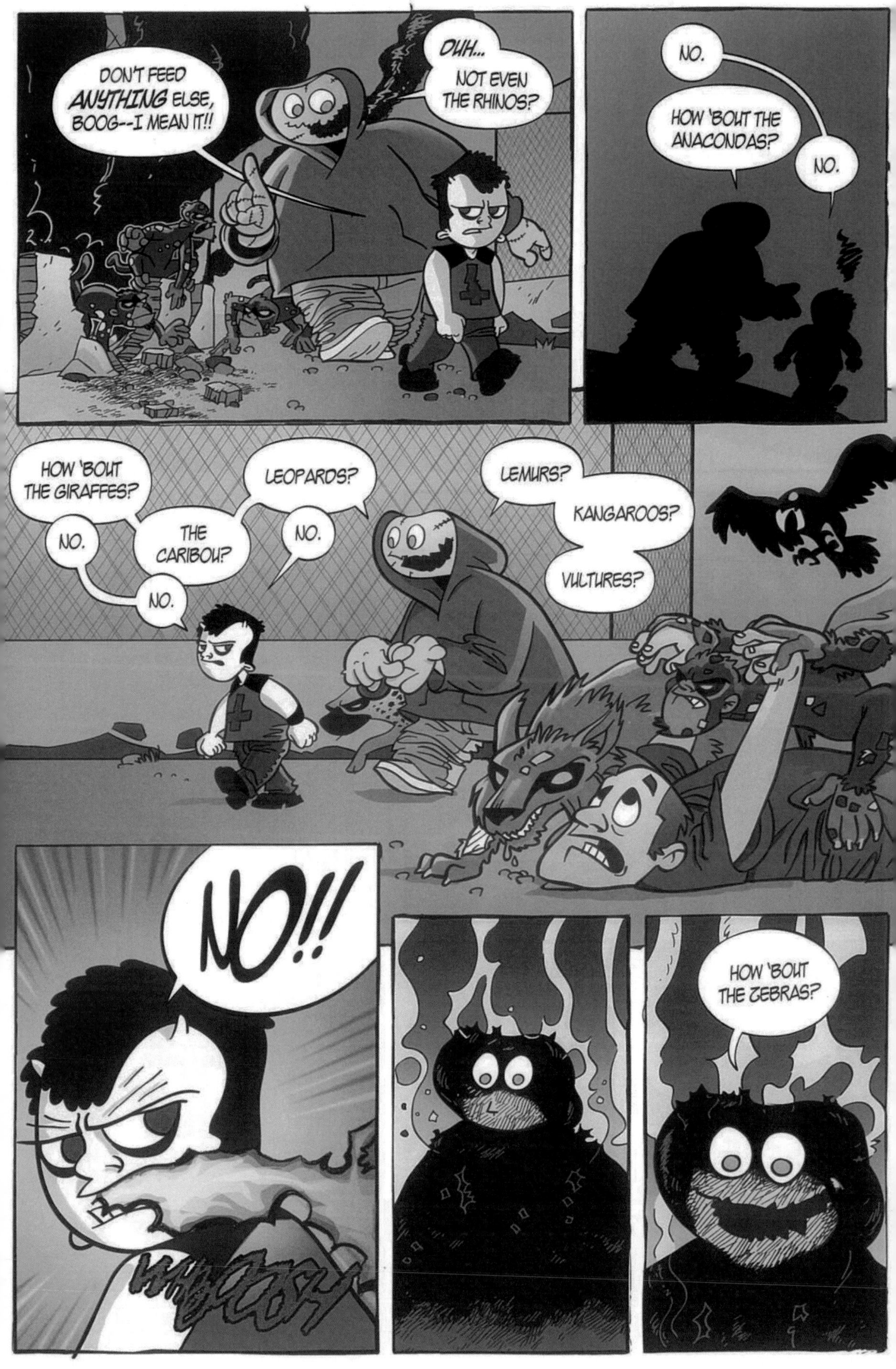
DON'T FEED *ANYTHING* ELSE, BOOG--I MEAN IT!!
OUH... NOT EVEN THE RHINOS?
NO.
HOW 'BOUT THE ANACONDAS?
NO.
HOW 'BOUT THE GIRAFFES?
NO.
THE CARIBOU?
NO.
LEOPARDS?
NO.
LEMURS?
KANGAROOS?
VULTURES?
NO!!
HOW 'BOUT THE ZEBRAS?

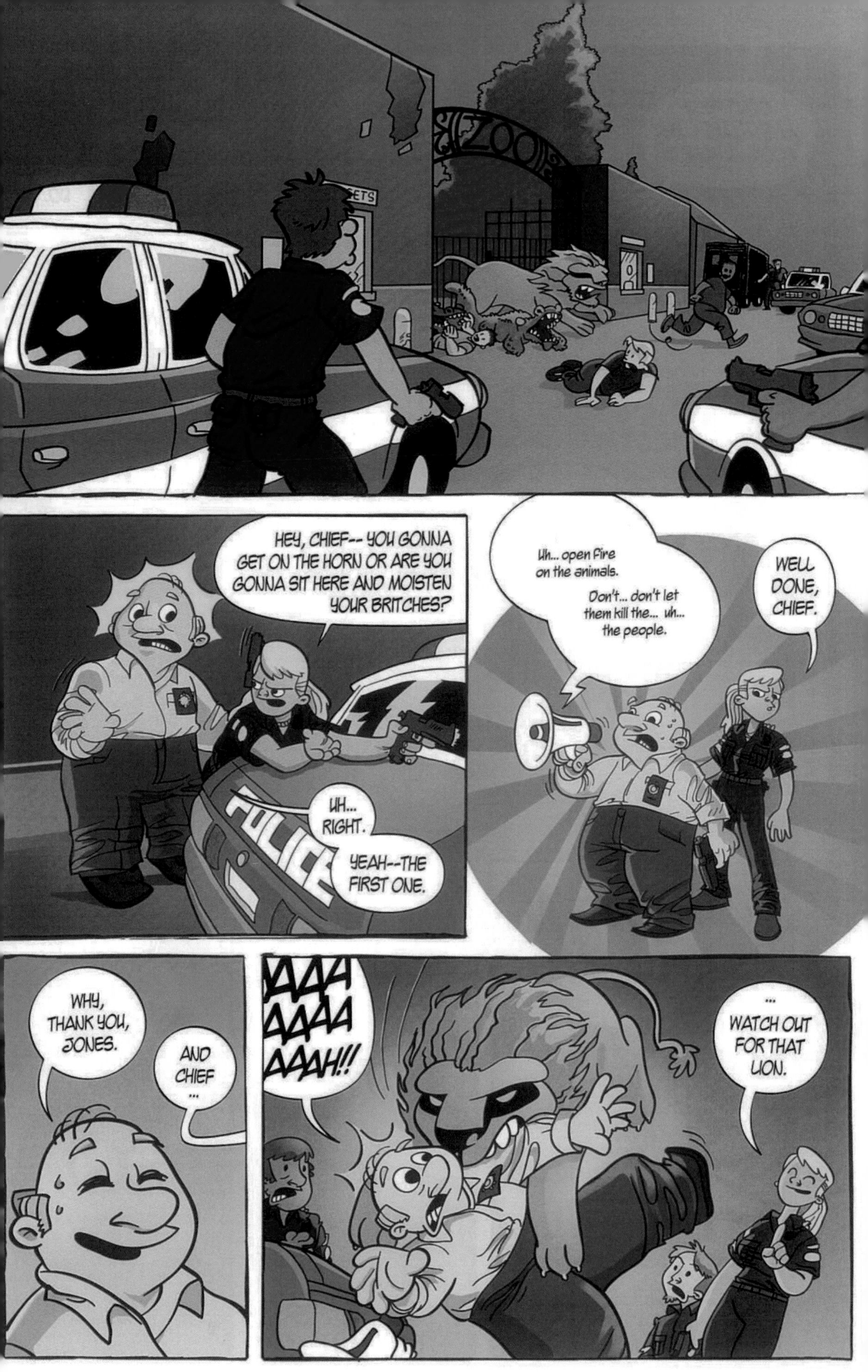
ZOO
TICKETS
HEY, CHIEF-- YOU GONNA GET ON THE HORN OR ARE YOU GONNA SIT HERE AND MOISTEN YOUR BRITCHES?
UH... RIGHT.
YEAH--THE FIRST ONE.
POLICE
Uh... open fire on the animals.
Don't... don't let them kill the... uh... the people.
WELL DONE, CHIEF.
WHY, THANK YOU, JONES.
AND CHIEF ...
AAAA AAAA AAAH!!
... WATCH OUT FOR THAT LION.

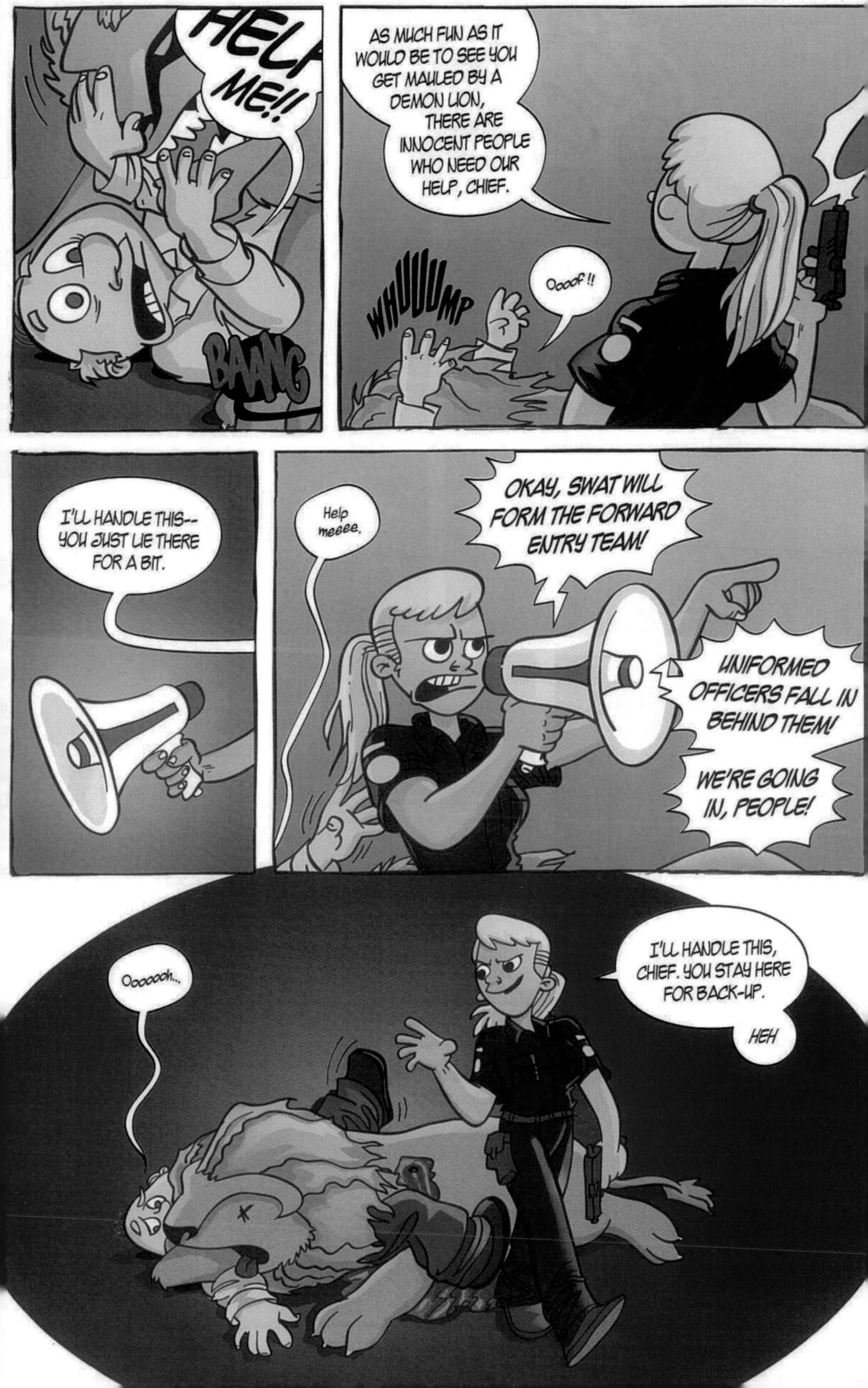
HELP ME!!
BAANG
AS MUCH FUN AS IT WOULD BE TO SEE YOU GET MAULED BY A DEMON LION,
THERE ARE INNOCENT PEOPLE WHO NEED OUR HELP, CHIEF.
WHUUUMP
Oooof !!
I'LL HANDLE THIS-- YOU JUST LIE THERE FOR A BIT.
Help meeee.
OKAY, SWAT WILL FORM THE FORWARD ENTRY TEAM!
UNIFORMED OFFICERS FALL IN BEHIND THEM!
WE'RE GOING IN, PEOPLE!
Ooooooh...
I'LL HANDLE THIS, CHIEF. YOU STAY HERE FOR BACK-UP.
HEH

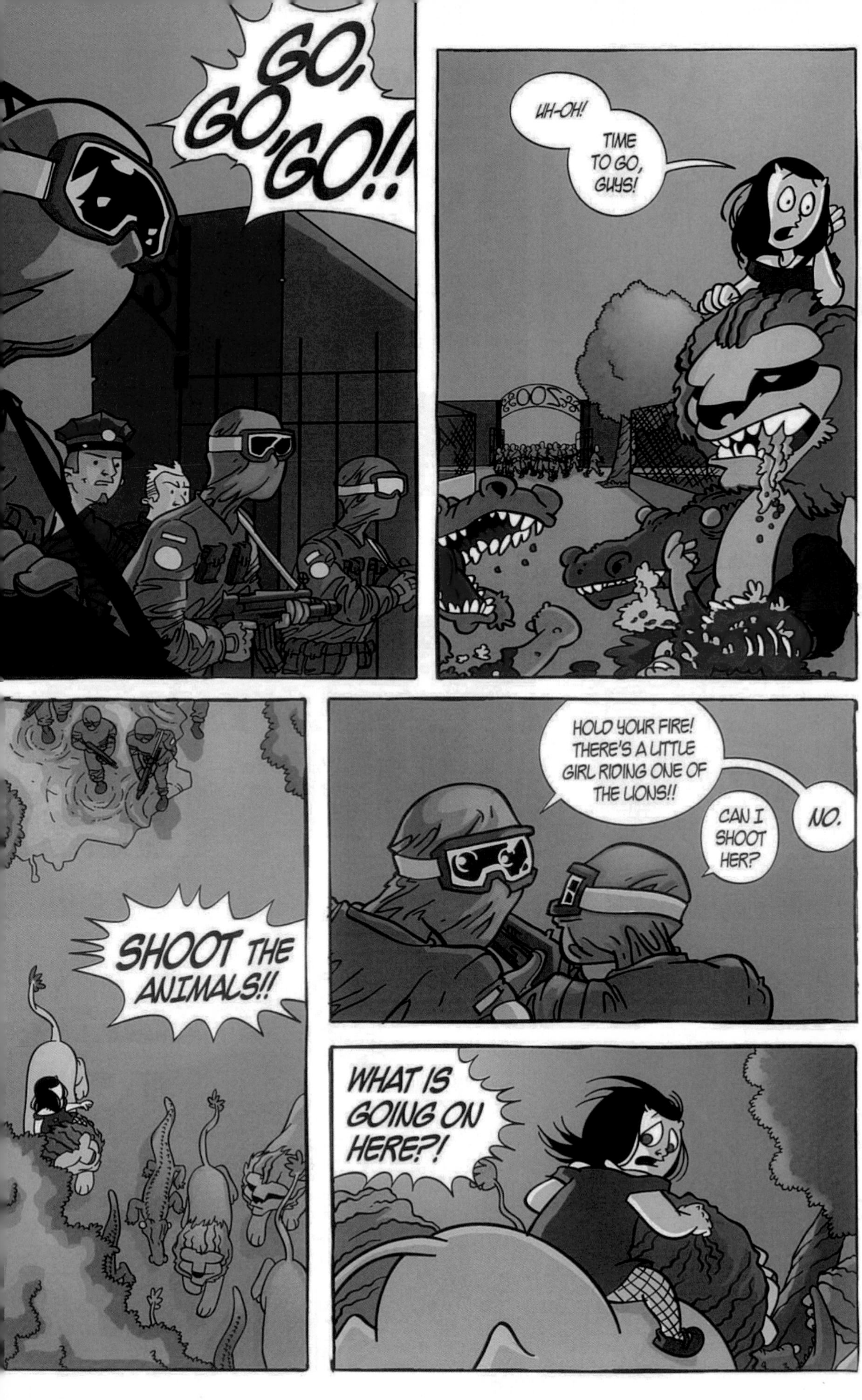
GO, GO, GO!!
UH-OH!
TIME TO GO, GUYS!
SHOOT THE ANIMALS!!
HOLD YOUR FIRE! THERE'S A LITTLE GIRL RIDING ONE OF THE LIONS!!
CAN I SHOOT HER?
NO.
WHAT IS GOING ON HERE?!

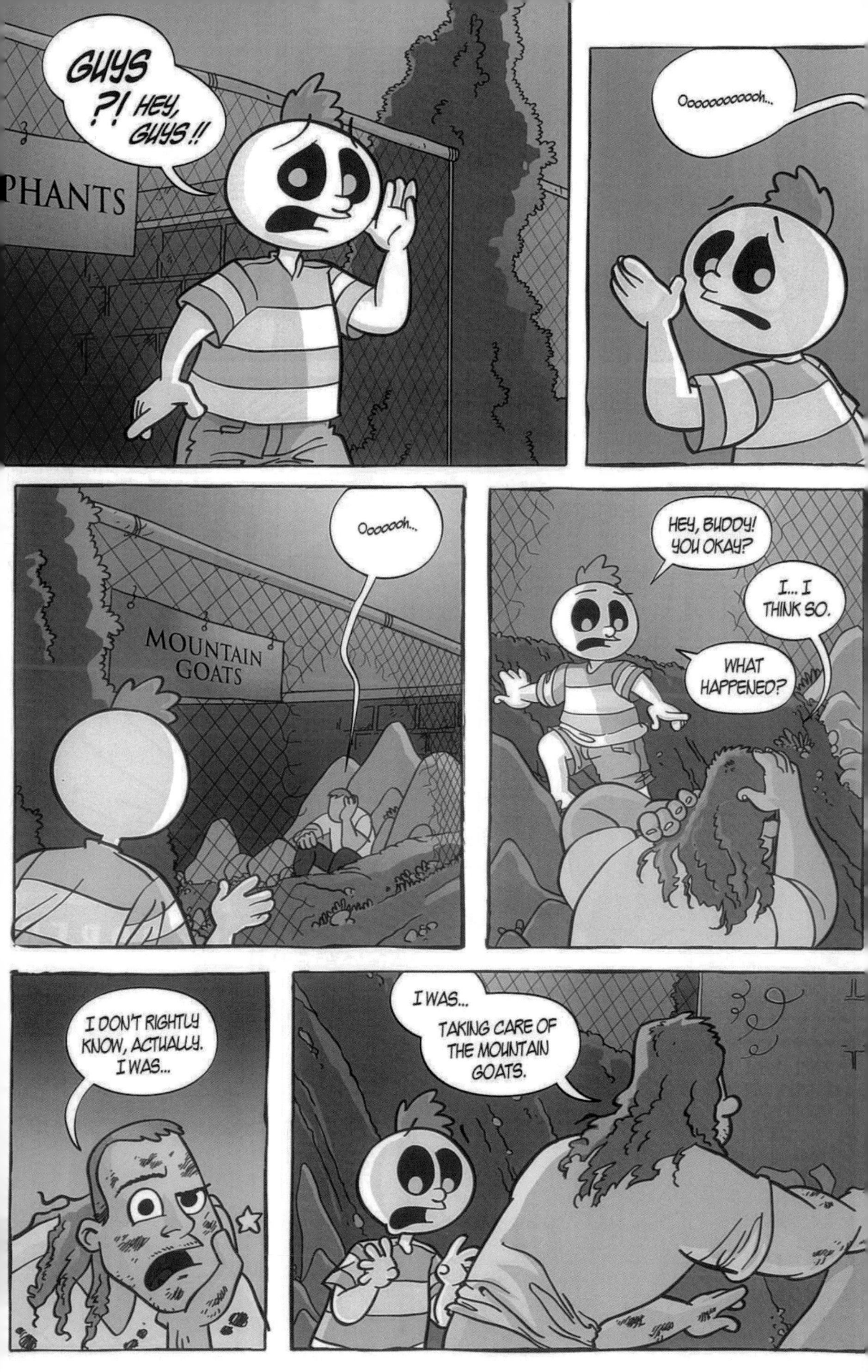
GUYS ?! HEY, GUYS !!
PHANTS
Oooooooooooh...
MOUNTAIN GOATS
Oooooh...
HEY, BUDDY! YOU OKAY?
I... I THINK SO.
WHAT HAPPENED?
I DON'T RIGHTLY KNOW, ACTUALLY. I WAS...
I WAS...
TAKING CARE OF THE MOUNTAIN GOATS.

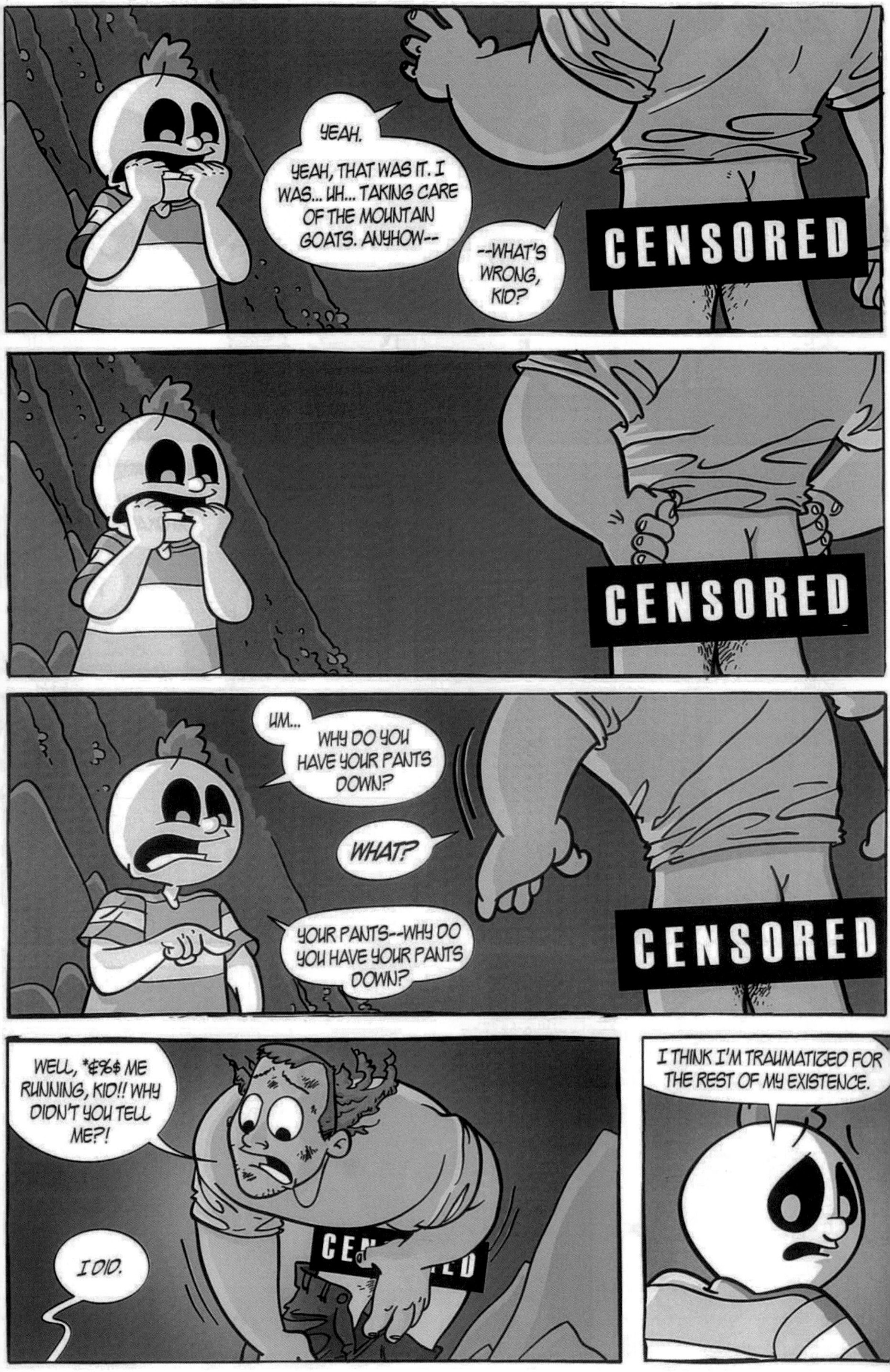
YEAH.
YEAH, THAT WAS IT. I WAS... UH... TAKING CARE OF THE MOUNTAIN GOATS. ANYHOW--
--WHAT'S WRONG, KID?
CENSORED
CENSORED
UM...
WHY DO YOU HAVE YOUR PANTS DOWN?
WHAT?
YOUR PANTS--WHY DO YOU HAVE YOUR PANTS DOWN?
CENSORED
WELL, *¢%$ ME RUNNING, KID!! WHY DIDN'T YOU TELL ME?!
I DID.
I THINK I'M TRAUMATIZED FOR THE REST OF MY EXISTENCE.

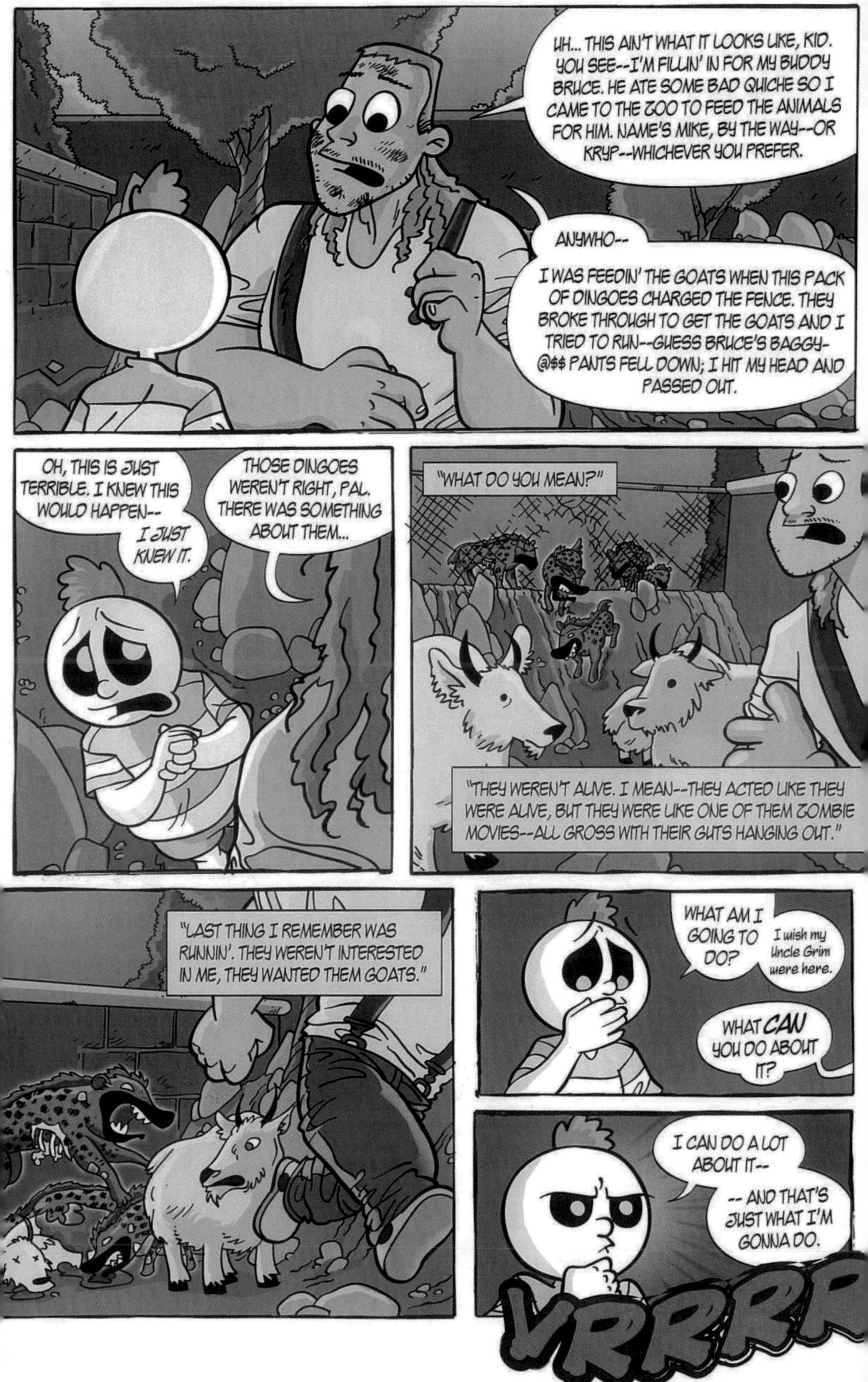
UH... THIS AIN'T WHAT IT LOOKS LIKE, KID. YOU SEE--I'M FILLIN' IN FOR MY BUDDY BRUCE. HE ATE SOME BAD QUICHE SO I CAME TO THE ZOO TO FEED THE ANIMALS FOR HIM. NAME'S MIKE, BY THE WAY--OR KRYP--WHICHEVER YOU PREFER.
ANYWHO--
I WAS FEEDIN' THE GOATS WHEN THIS PACK OF DINGOES CHARGED THE FENCE. THEY BROKE THROUGH TO GET THE GOATS AND I TRIED TO RUN--GUESS BRUCE'S BAGGY-@$$ PANTS FELL DOWN; I HIT MY HEAD AND PASSED OUT.
OH, THIS IS JUST TERRIBLE. I KNEW THIS WOULD HAPPEN--
I JUST KNEW IT.
THOSE DINGOES WEREN'T RIGHT, PAL. THERE WAS SOMETHING ABOUT THEM...
"WHAT DO YOU MEAN?"
"THEY WEREN'T ALIVE. I MEAN--THEY ACTED LIKE THEY WERE ALIVE, BUT THEY WERE LIKE ONE OF THEM ZOMBIE MOVIES--ALL GROSS WITH THEIR GUTS HANGING OUT."
"LAST THING I REMEMBER WAS RUNNIN'. THEY WEREN'T INTERESTED IN ME, THEY WANTED THEM GOATS."
WHAT AM I GOING TO DO?
I wish my Uncle Grim were here.
WHAT CAN YOU DO ABOUT IT?
I CAN DO A LOT ABOUT IT--
--AND THAT'S JUST WHAT I'M GONNA DO.
VRRRR

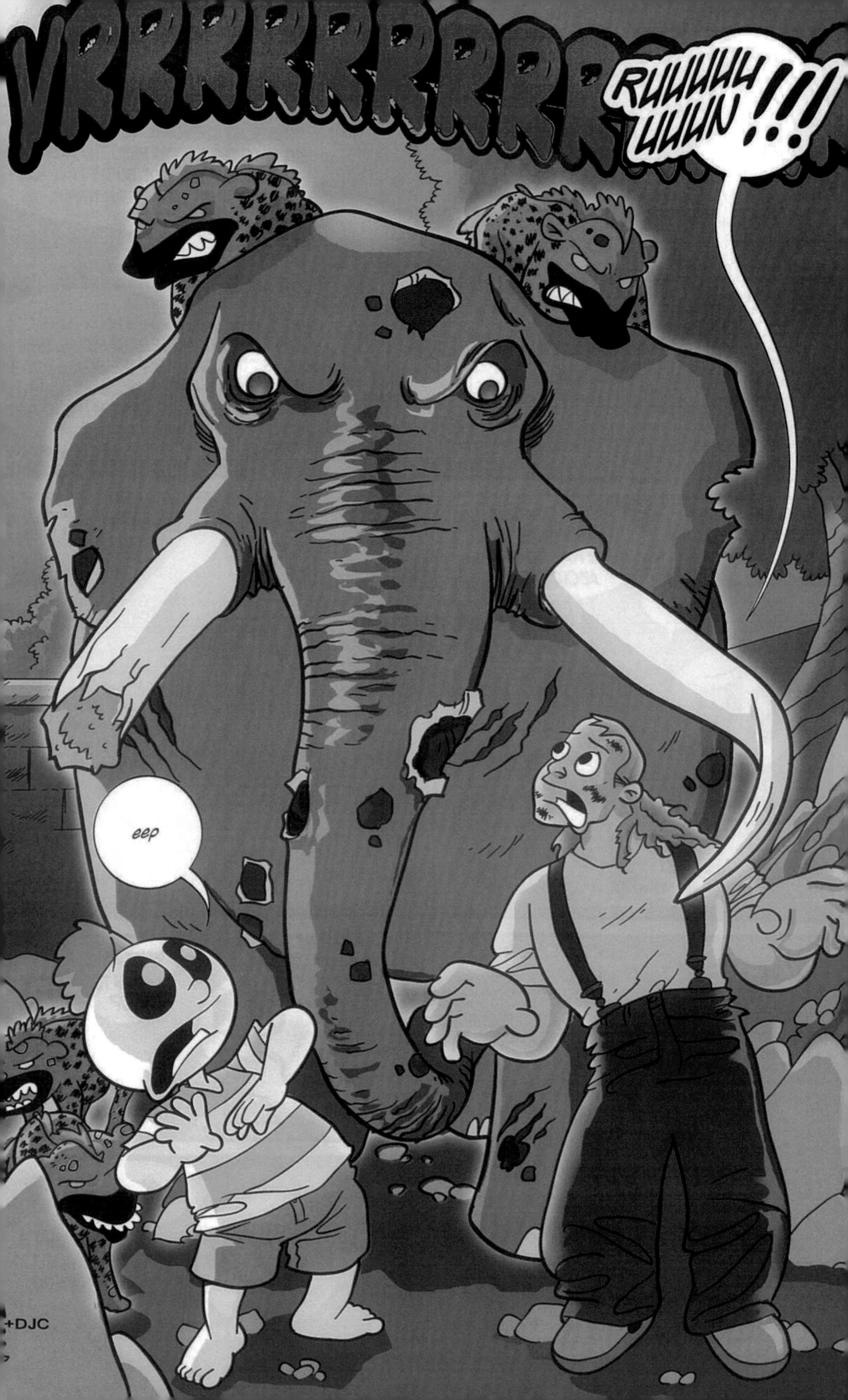
VRRRRRRRRRR
RUUUUU
UUUN!!!
eep
+DJC

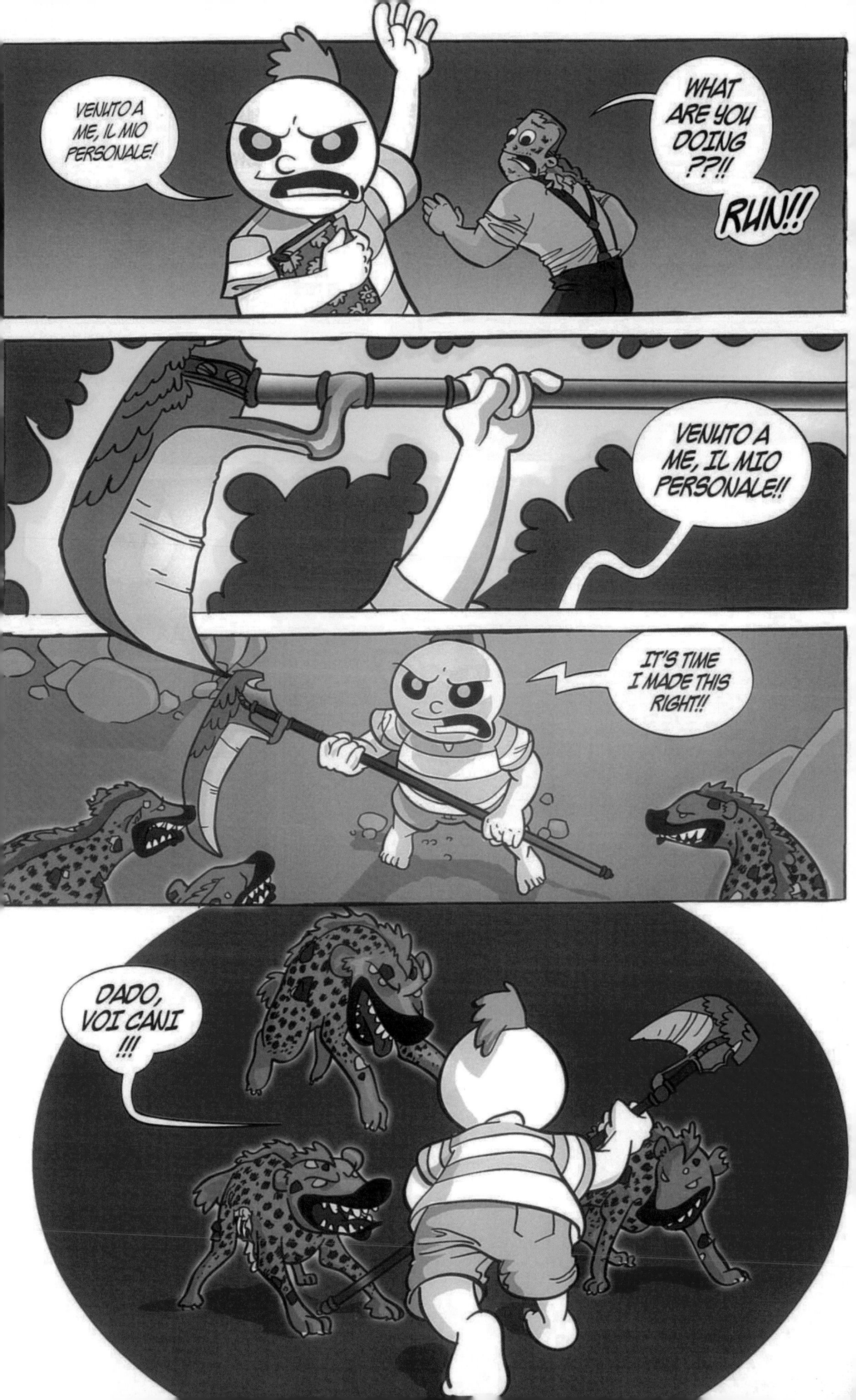
VENUTO A ME, IL MIO PERSONALE!
WHAT ARE YOU DOING ??!!
RUN!!
VENUTO A ME, IL MIO PERSONALE!!
IT'S TIME I MADE THIS RIGHT!!
DADO, VOI CANI !!!

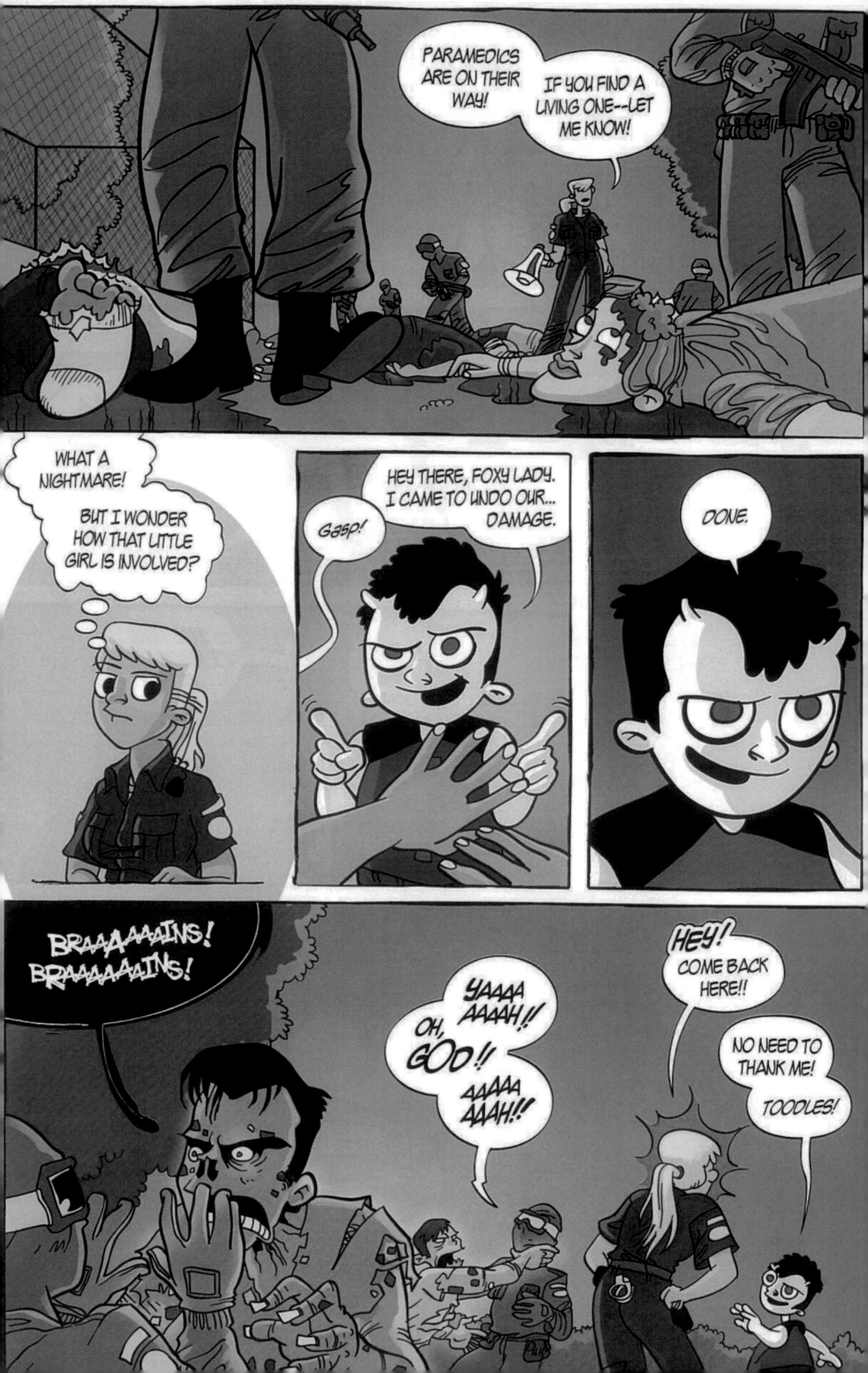
PARAMEDICS ARE ON THEIR WAY!
IF YOU FIND A LIVING ONE--LET ME KNOW!
WHAT A NIGHTMARE!
BUT I WONDER HOW THAT LITTLE GIRL IS INVOLVED?
HEY THERE, FOXY LADY. I CAME TO UNDO OUR... DAMAGE.
Gasp!
DONE.
BRAAAAAAINS! BRAAAAAAINS!
YAAAA AAAAH!!
OH, GOD!!
AAAAA AAAH!!
HEY! COME BACK HERE!!
NO NEED TO THANK ME!
TOODLES!

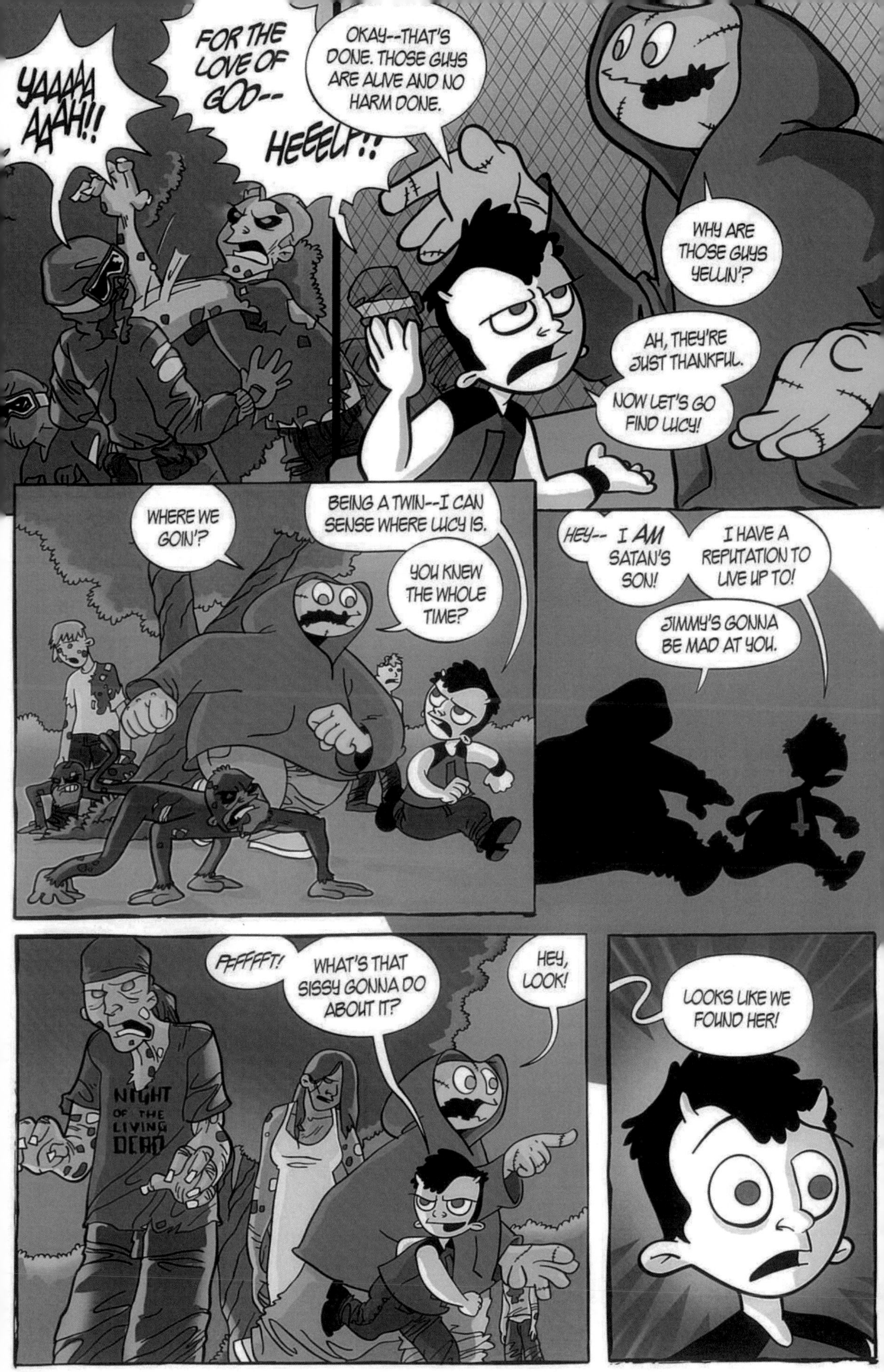
YAAAAA AAAH!!
FOR THE LOVE OF GOD--
HEEELP!!
OKAY--THAT'S DONE. THOSE GUYS ARE ALIVE AND NO HARM DONE.
WHY ARE THOSE GUYS YELLIN'?
AH, THEY'RE JUST THANKFUL.
NOW LET'S GO FIND LUCY!
WHERE WE GOIN'?
BEING A TWIN--I CAN SENSE WHERE LUCY IS.
YOU KNEW THE WHOLE TIME?
HEY-- I AM SATAN'S SON!
I HAVE A REPUTATION TO LIVE UP TO!
JIMMY'S GONNA BE MAD AT YOU.
PFFFFFT!
WHAT'S THAT SISSY GONNA DO ABOUT IT?
HEY, LOOK!
NIGHT OF THE LIVING DEAD
LOOKS LIKE WE FOUND HER!

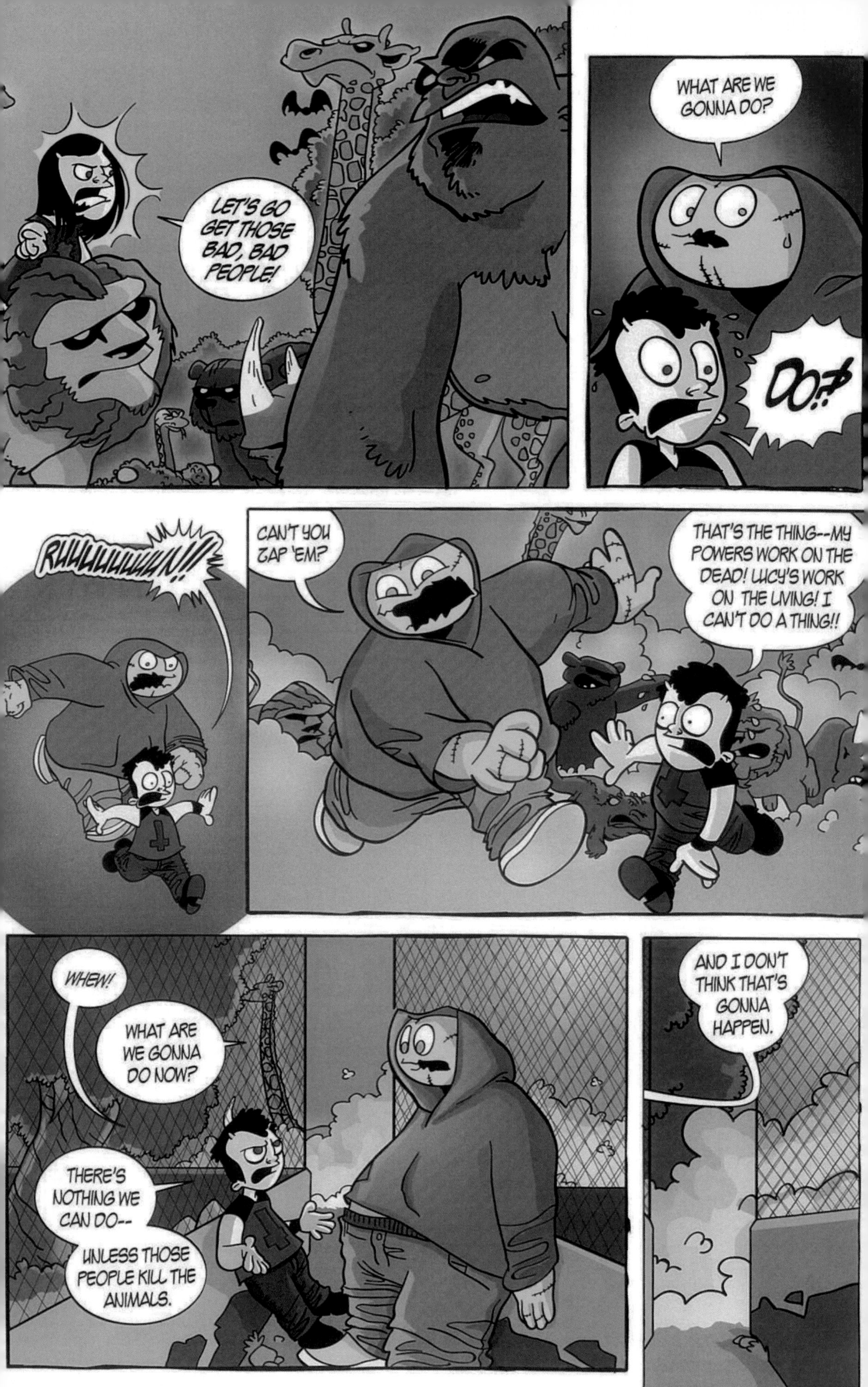
LET'S GO GET THOSE BAD, BAD PEOPLE!
WHAT ARE WE GONNA DO?
DO?!?
RUUUUUUUUUN!!
CAN'T YOU ZAP 'EM?
THAT'S THE THING--MY POWERS WORK ON THE DEAD! LUCY'S WORK ON THE LIVING! I CAN'T DO A THING!!
WHEW!
WHAT ARE WE GONNA DO NOW?
THERE'S NOTHING WE CAN DO--
UNLESS THOSE PEOPLE KILL THE ANIMALS.
AND I DON'T THINK THAT'S GONNA HAPPEN.

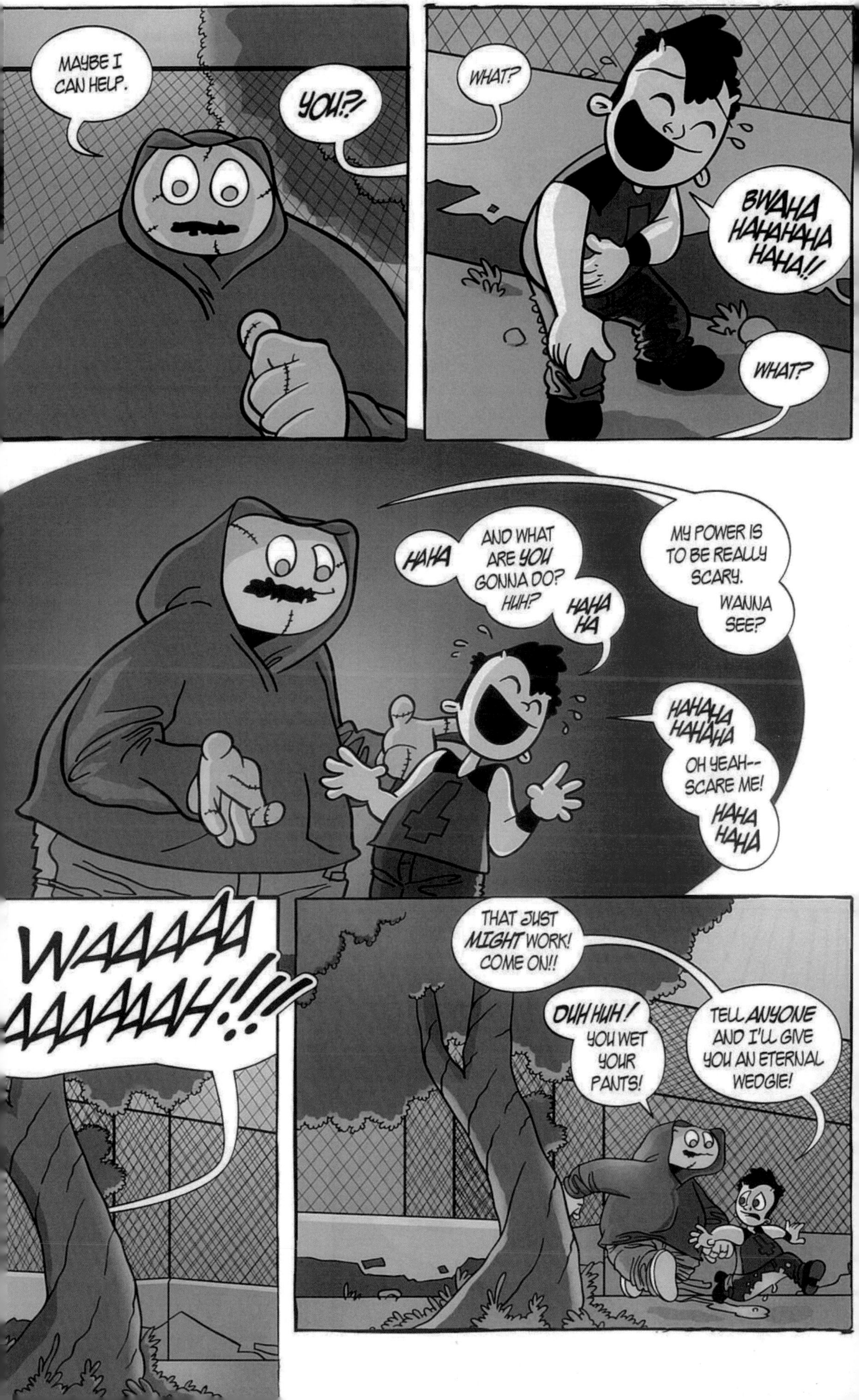
MAYBE I CAN HELP.
YOU!?!
WHAT?
BWAHA HAHAHAHA HAHA!!
WHAT?
MY POWER IS TO BE REALLY SCARY.
WANNA SEE?
HAHA
AND WHAT ARE YOU GONNA DO? HUH?
HAHA HA
HAHAHA HAHAHA
OH YEAH-- SCARE ME!
HAHA HAHA
WAAAAA AAAAAAH!!!
THAT JUST MIGHT WORK! COME ON!!
DUH HUH! YOU WET YOUR PANTS!
TELL ANYONE AND I'LL GIVE YOU AN ETERNAL WEDGIE!

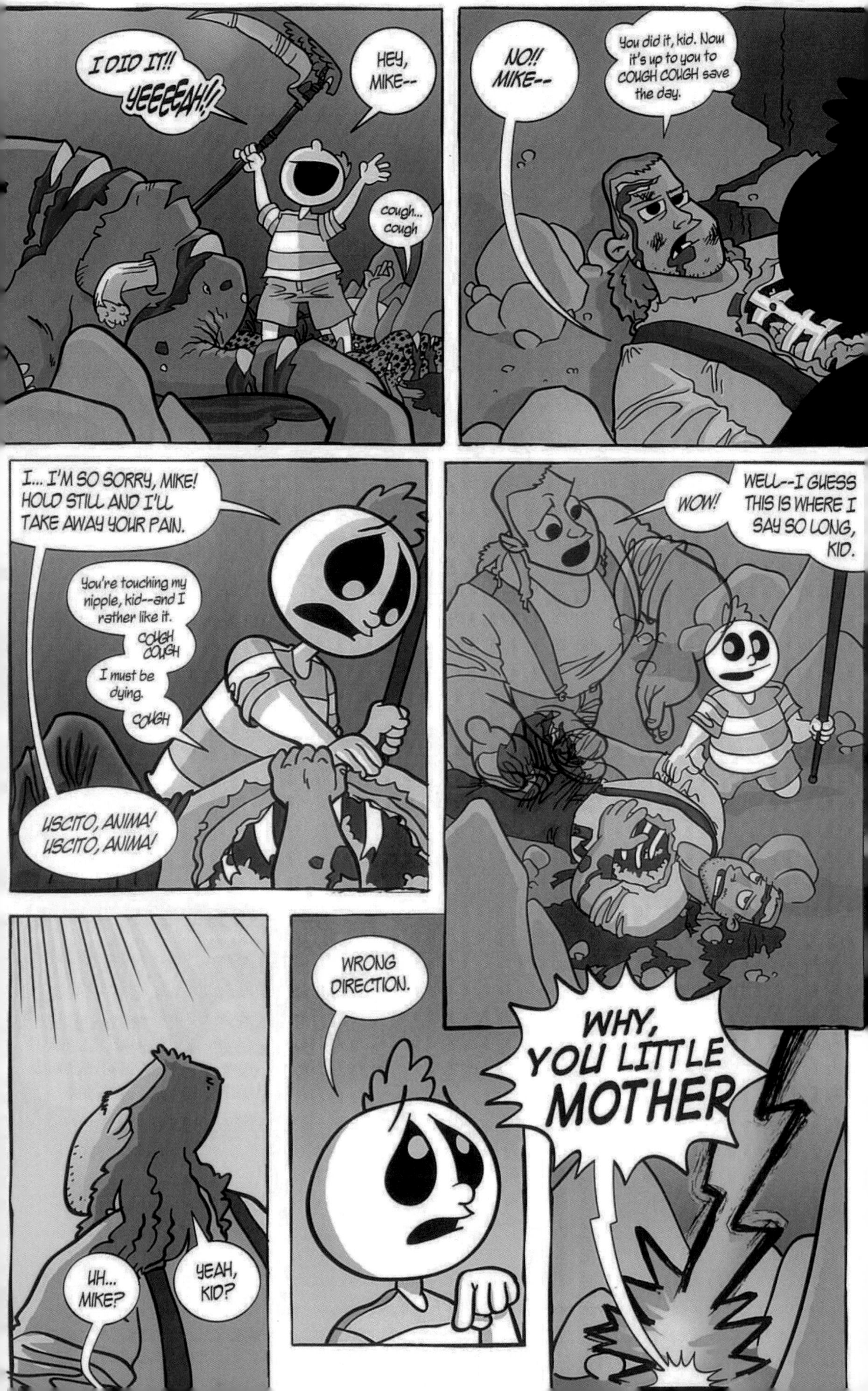
I DID IT!!
YEEEEAH!!
HEY, MIKE--
cough... cough
NO!! MIKE--
You did it, kid. Now it's up to you to COUGH COUGH save the day.
I... I'M SO SORRY, MIKE! HOLD STILL AND I'LL TAKE AWAY YOUR PAIN.
You're touching my nipple, kid--and I rather like it.
COUGH COUGH
I must be dying.
COUGH
USCITO, ANIMA! USCITO, ANIMA!
WOW!
WELL--I GUESS THIS IS WHERE I SAY SO LONG, KID.
UH... MIKE?
YEAH, KID?
WRONG DIRECTION.
WHY, YOU LITTLE MOTHER

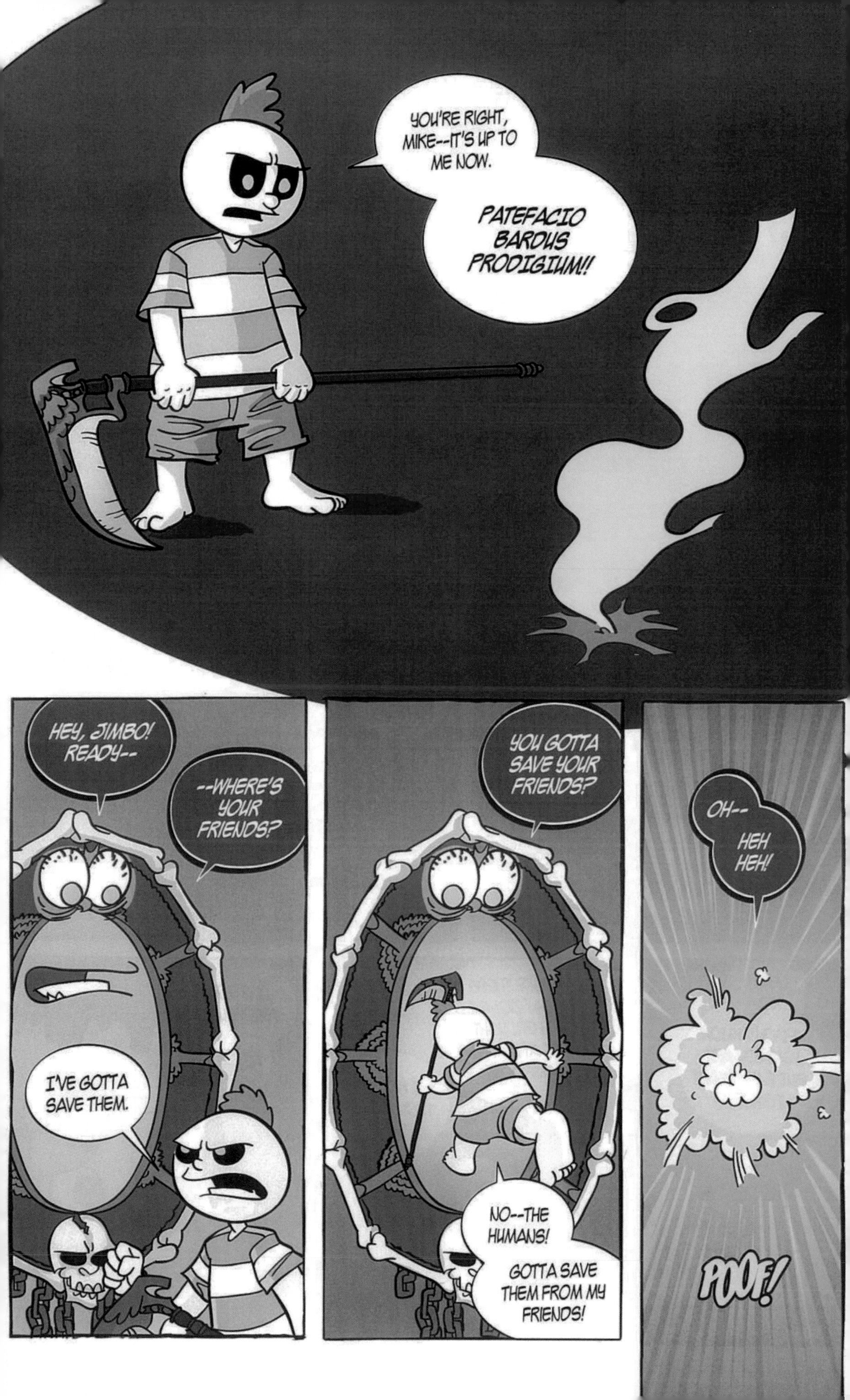
YOU'RE RIGHT, MIKE--IT'S UP TO ME NOW.
PATEFACIO BARDUS PRODIGIUM!!
HEY, JIMBO! READY--
--WHERE'S YOUR FRIENDS?
I'VE GOTTA SAVE THEM.
YOU GOTTA SAVE YOUR FRIENDS?
NO--THE HUMANS!
GOTTA SAVE THEM FROM MY FRIENDS!
OH--
HEH HEH!
POOF!

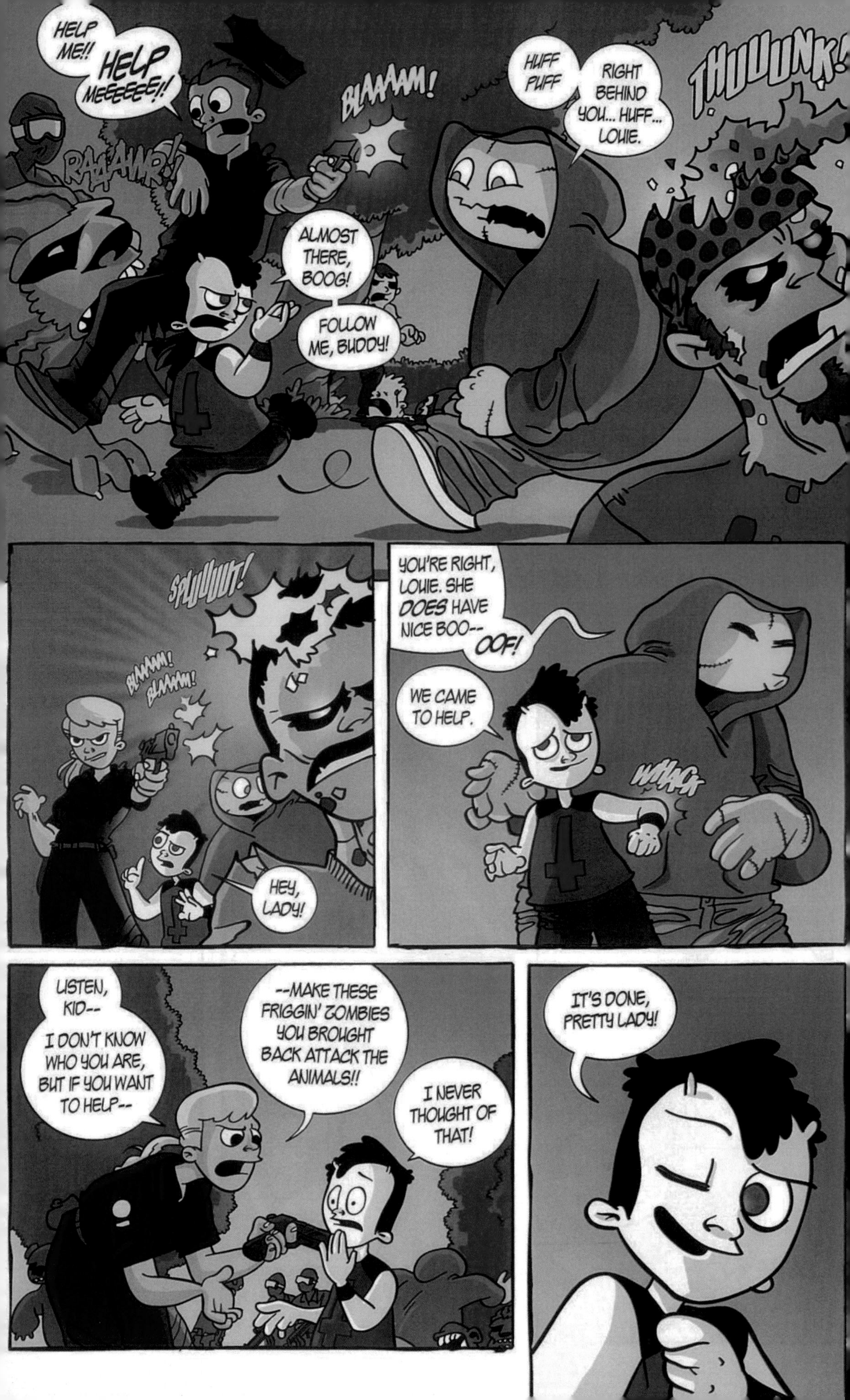
HELP ME!! HELP MEEEEEE!!
RAAAWR!
BLAAAAM!
ALMOST THERE, BOOG!
FOLLOW ME, BUDDY!
HUFF PUFF
RIGHT BEHIND YOU... HUFF... LOUIE.
THUUUNK!
SPLUUUUT!
BLAAAAM! BLAAAAM!
HEY, LADY!
YOU'RE RIGHT, LOUIE. SHE DOES HAVE NICE BOO-- OOF!
WE CAME TO HELP.
WHACK
LISTEN, KID--
I DON'T KNOW WHO YOU ARE, BUT IF YOU WANT TO HELP--
--MAKE THESE FRIGGIN' ZOMBIES YOU BROUGHT BACK ATTACK THE ANIMALS!!
I NEVER THOUGHT OF THAT!
IT'S DONE, PRETTY LADY!

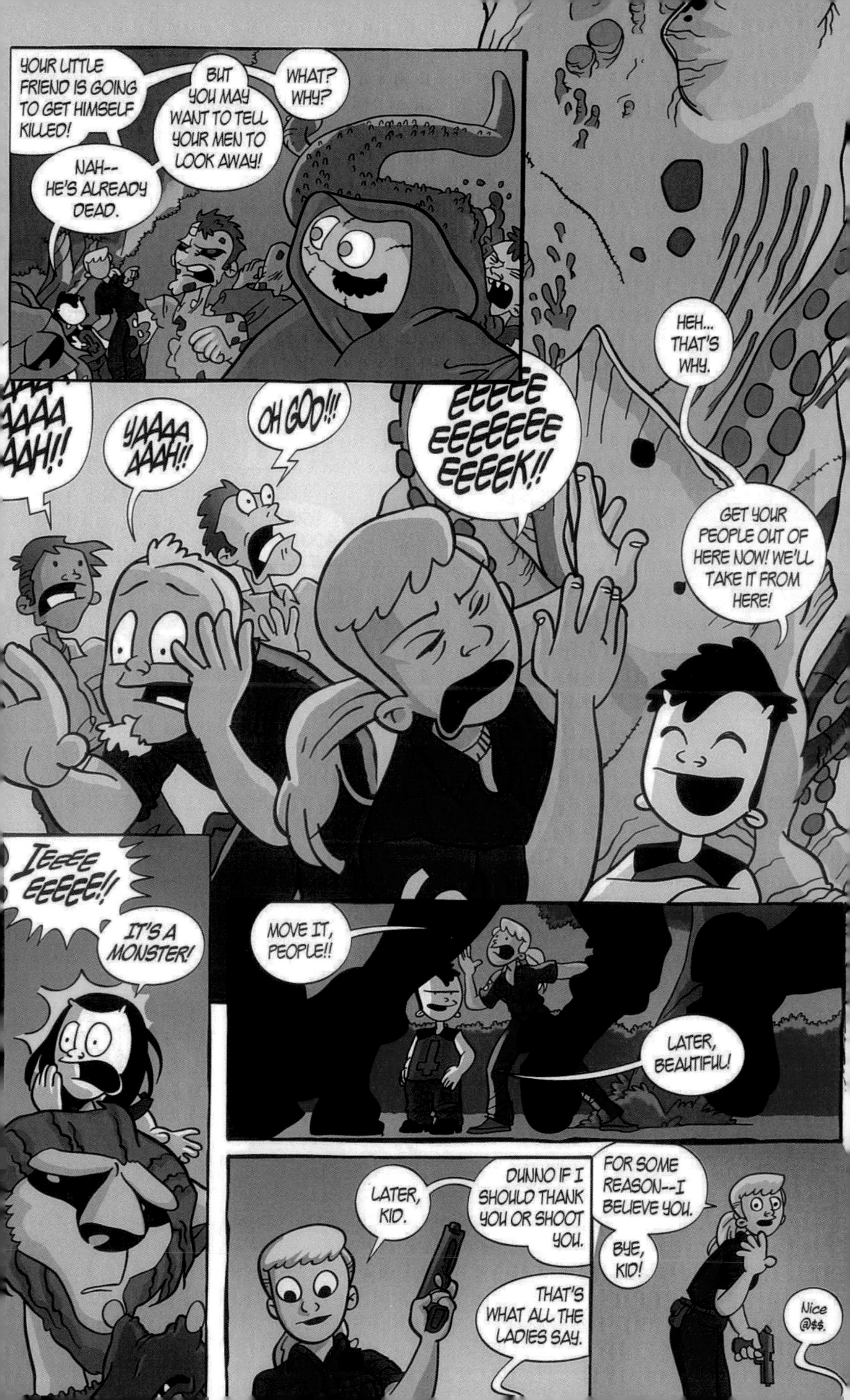
YOUR LITTLE FRIEND IS GOING TO GET HIMSELF KILLED!
NAH-- HE'S ALREADY DEAD.
BUT YOU MAY WANT TO TELL YOUR MEN TO LOOK AWAY!
WHAT? WHY?
HEH... THAT'S WHY.
AAAH!!
YAAAA AAAH!!
OH GOD!!!
EEEEE EEEEEEE EEEEEK!!
GET YOUR PEOPLE OUT OF HERE NOW! WE'LL TAKE IT FROM HERE!
IEEEE EEEEE!!
IT'S A MONSTER!
MOVE IT, PEOPLE!!
LATER, BEAUTIFUL!
LATER, KID.
DUNNO IF I SHOULD THANK YOU OR SHOOT YOU.
THAT'S WHAT ALL THE LADIES SAY.
FOR SOME REASON--I BELIEVE YOU.
BYE, KID!
Nice @$$.

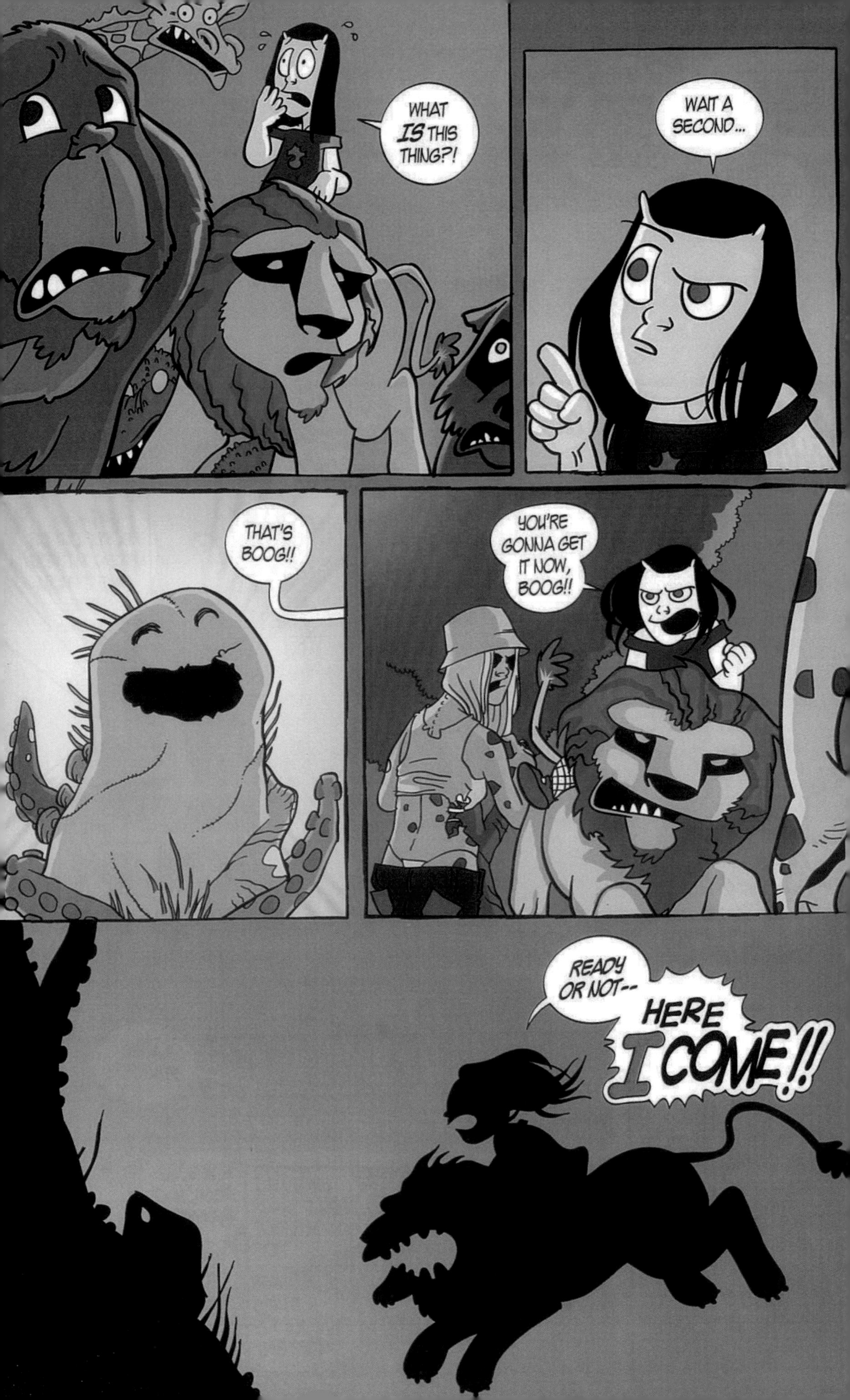
WHAT IS THIS THING?!
WAIT A SECOND...
THAT'S BOOG!!
YOU'RE GONNA GET IT NOW, BOOG!!
READY OR NOT--
HERE I COME!!

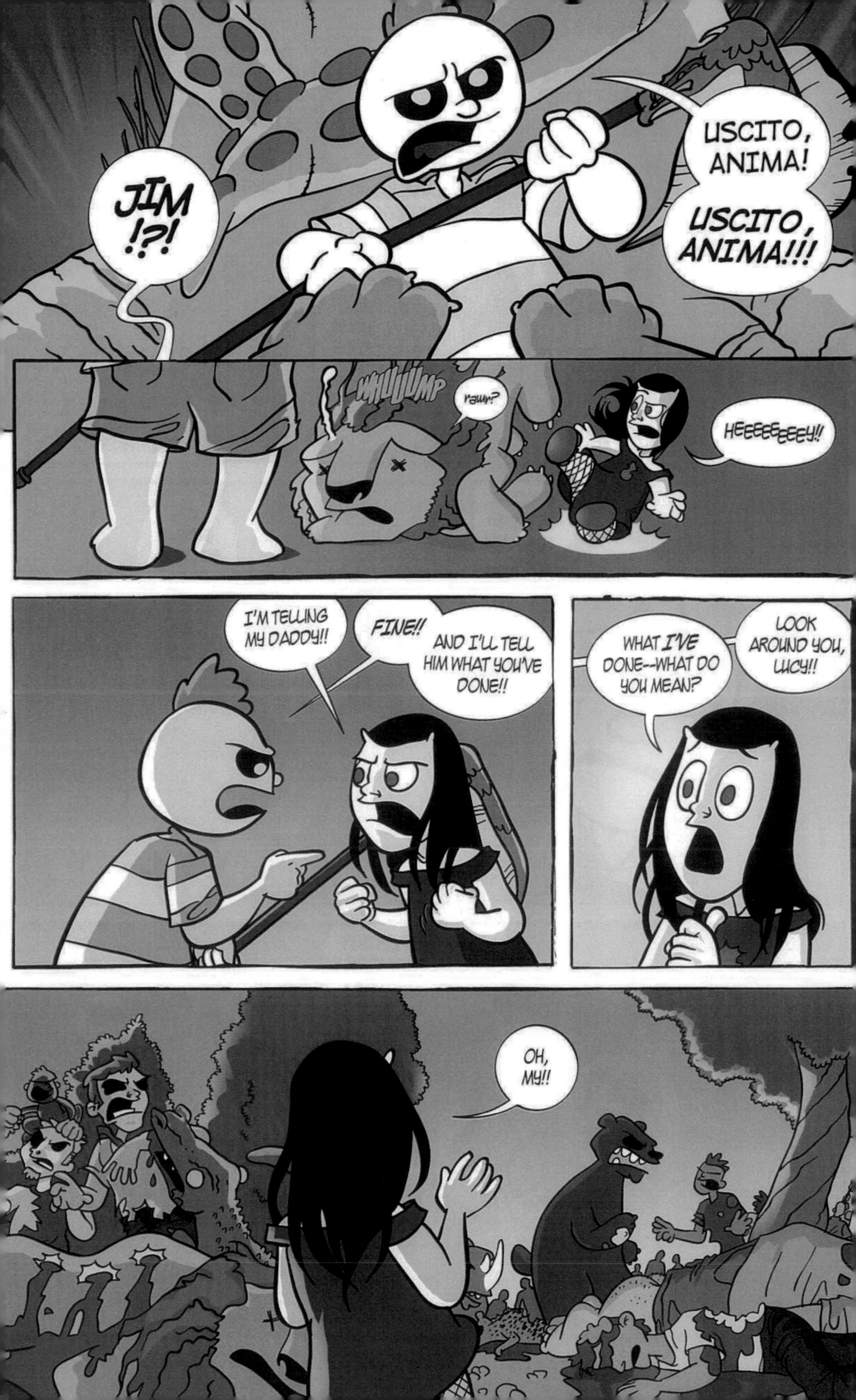
USCITO, ANIMA!
USCITO, ANIMA!!!
JIM !?!
WHUUUMP
rawr?
HEEEEEEEEEY!!
I'M TELLING MY DADDY!!
FINE!!
AND I'LL TELL HIM WHAT YOU'VE DONE!!
WHAT I'VE DONE--WHAT DO YOU MEAN?
LOOK AROUND YOU, LUCY!!
OH, MY!!

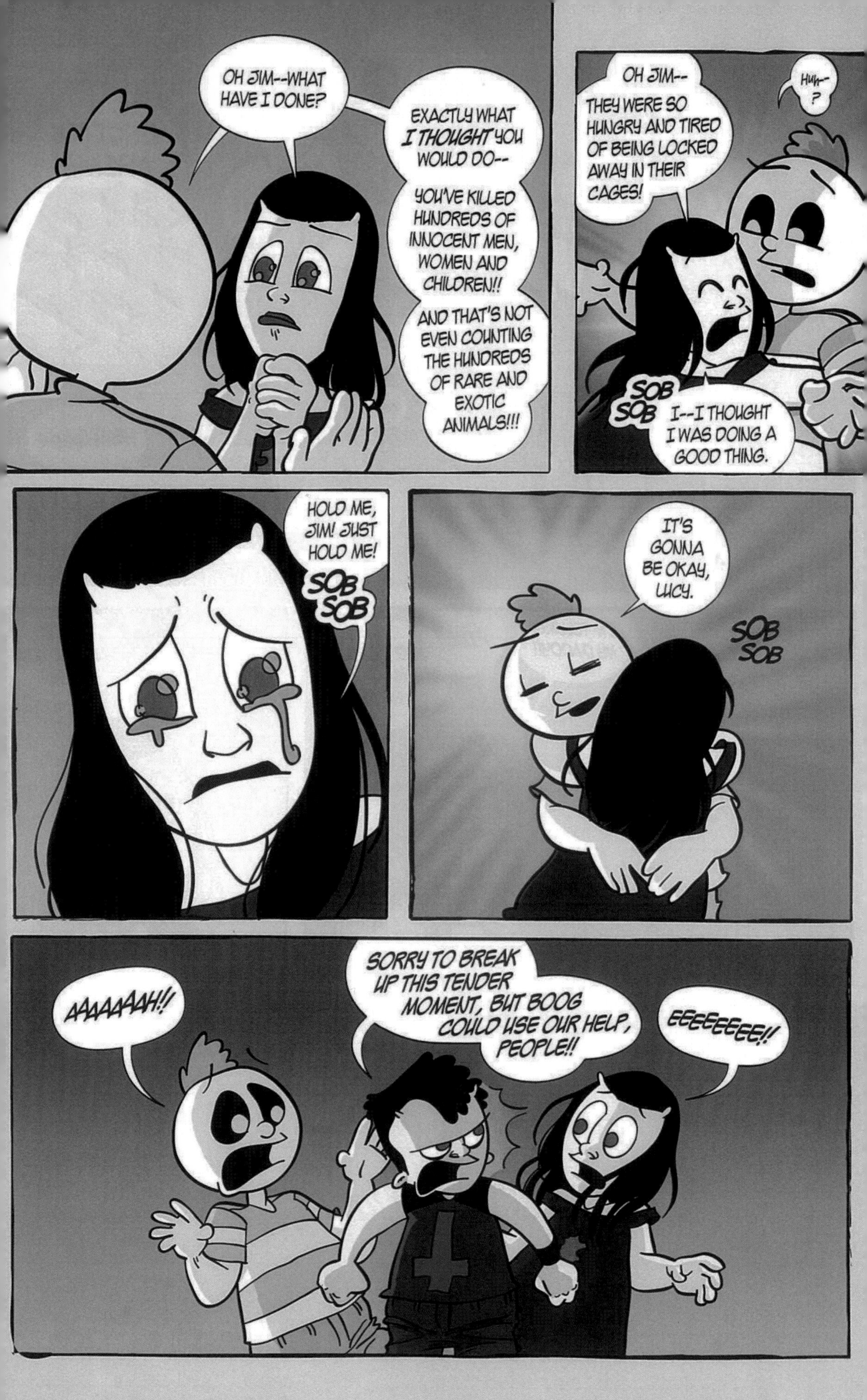

OH JIM--WHAT HAVE I DONE?
EXACTLY WHAT I THOUGHT YOU WOULD DO--
YOU'VE KILLED HUNDREDS OF INNOCENT MEN, WOMEN AND CHILDREN!!
AND THAT'S NOT EVEN COUNTING THE HUNDREDS OF RARE AND EXOTIC ANIMALS!!!
OH JIM--
THEY WERE SO HUNGRY AND TIRED OF BEING LOCKED AWAY IN THEIR CAGES!
HUH--?
SOB SOB
I--I THOUGHT I WAS DOING A GOOD THING.
HOLD ME, JIM! JUST HOLD ME!
SOB SOB
IT'S GONNA BE OKAY, LUCY.
SOB SOB
AAAAAAAH!!
SORRY TO BREAK UP THIS TENDER MOMENT, BUT BOOG COULD USE OUR HELP, PEOPLE!!
EEEEEEEEE!!

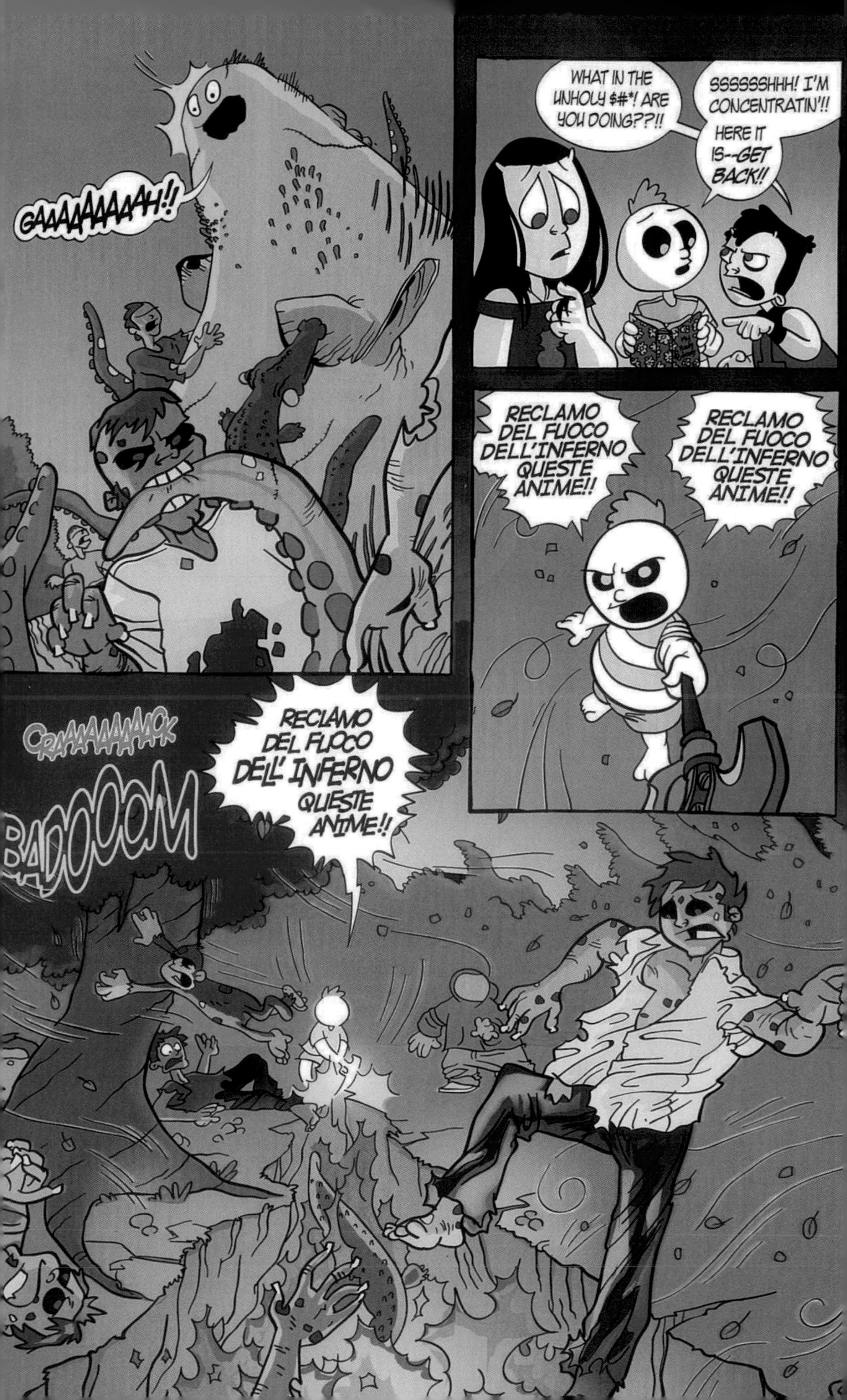
GAAAAAAAAAH!!
WHAT IN THE UNHOLY $#*! ARE YOU DOING??!!
SSSSSSHHH! I'M CONCENTRATIN'!!
HERE IT IS--GET BACK!!
RECLAMO DEL FUOCO DELL'INFERNO QUESTE ANIME!!
RECLAMO DEL FUOCO DELL'INFERNO QUESTE ANIME!!
CRAAAAAAAACK
BADOOOM
RECLAMO DEL FUOCO DELL' INFERNO QUESTE ANIME!!

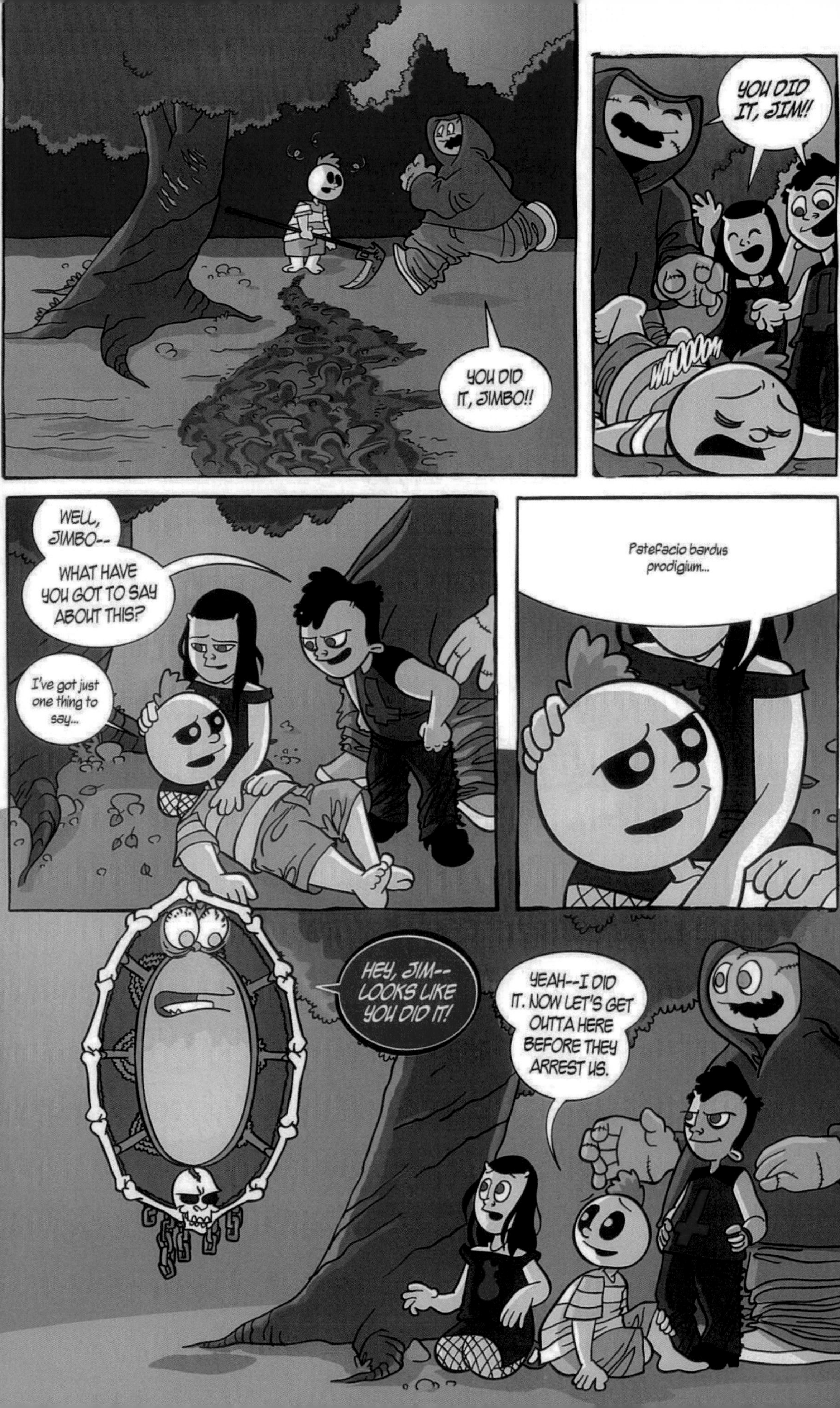
YOU DID IT, JIMBO!!
YOU DID IT, JIM!!
WHOOOOM
WELL, JIMBO--
WHAT HAVE YOU GOT TO SAY ABOUT THIS?
I've got just one thing to say...
Patefacio bardus prodigium...
HEY, JIM-- LOOKS LIKE YOU DID IT!
YEAH--I DID IT. NOW LET'S GET OUTTA HERE BEFORE THEY ARREST US.

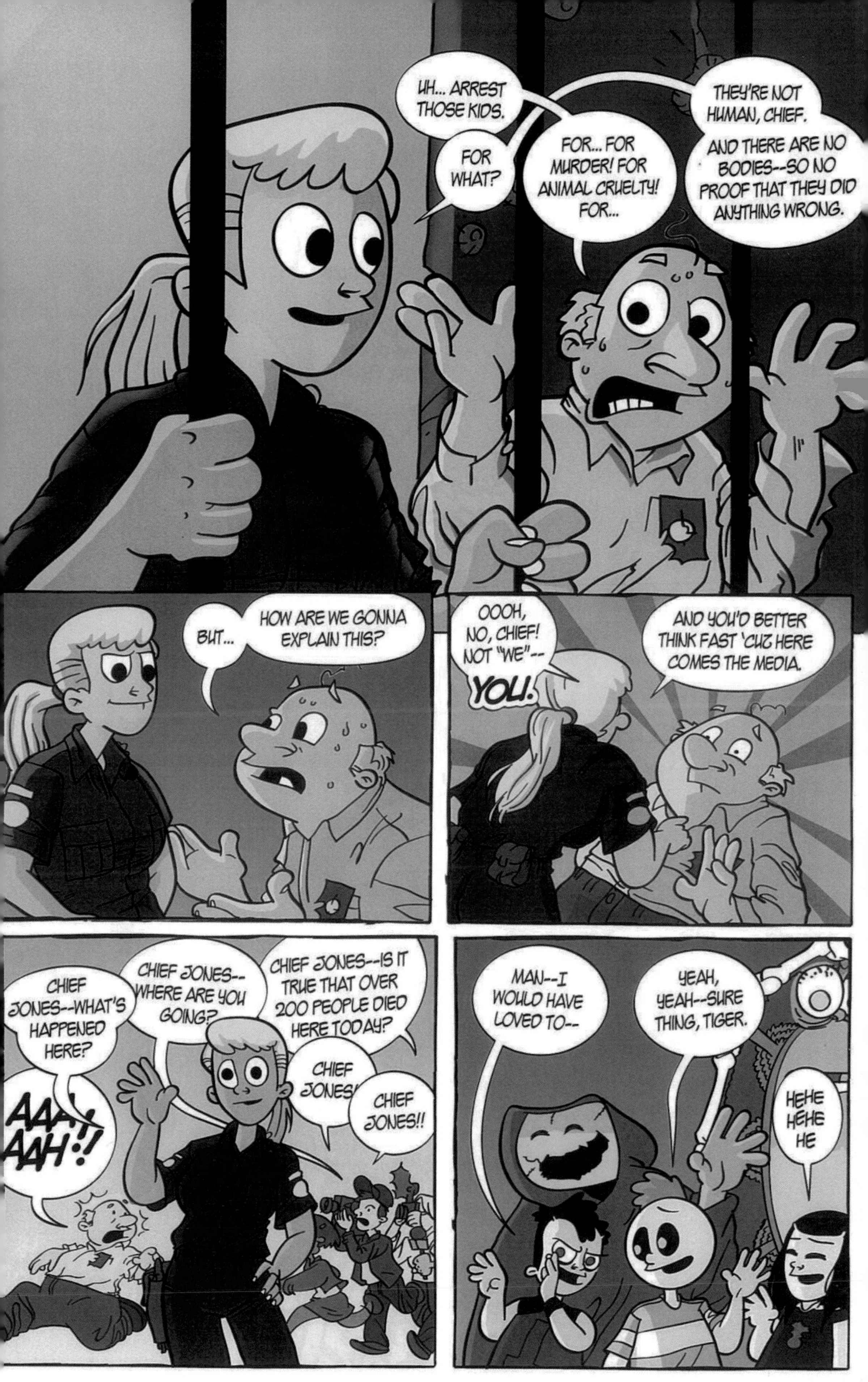
UH... ARREST THOSE KIDS.
FOR WHAT?
FOR... FOR MURDER! FOR ANIMAL CRUELTY! FOR...
THEY'RE NOT HUMAN, CHIEF.
AND THERE ARE NO BODIES--SO NO PROOF THAT THEY DID ANYTHING WRONG.
BUT...
HOW ARE WE GONNA EXPLAIN THIS?
OOOH, NO, CHIEF! NOT "WE"--
YOU!
AND YOU'D BETTER THINK FAST 'CUZ HERE COMES THE MEDIA.
CHIEF JONES--WHAT'S HAPPENED HERE?
CHIEF JONES--WHERE ARE YOU GOING?
CHIEF JONES--IS IT TRUE THAT OVER 200 PEOPLE DIED HERE TODAY?
CHIEF JONES!
CHIEF JONES!!
MAN--I WOULD HAVE LOVED TO--
YEAH, YEAH--SURE THING, TIGER.
HEHE HEHE HE

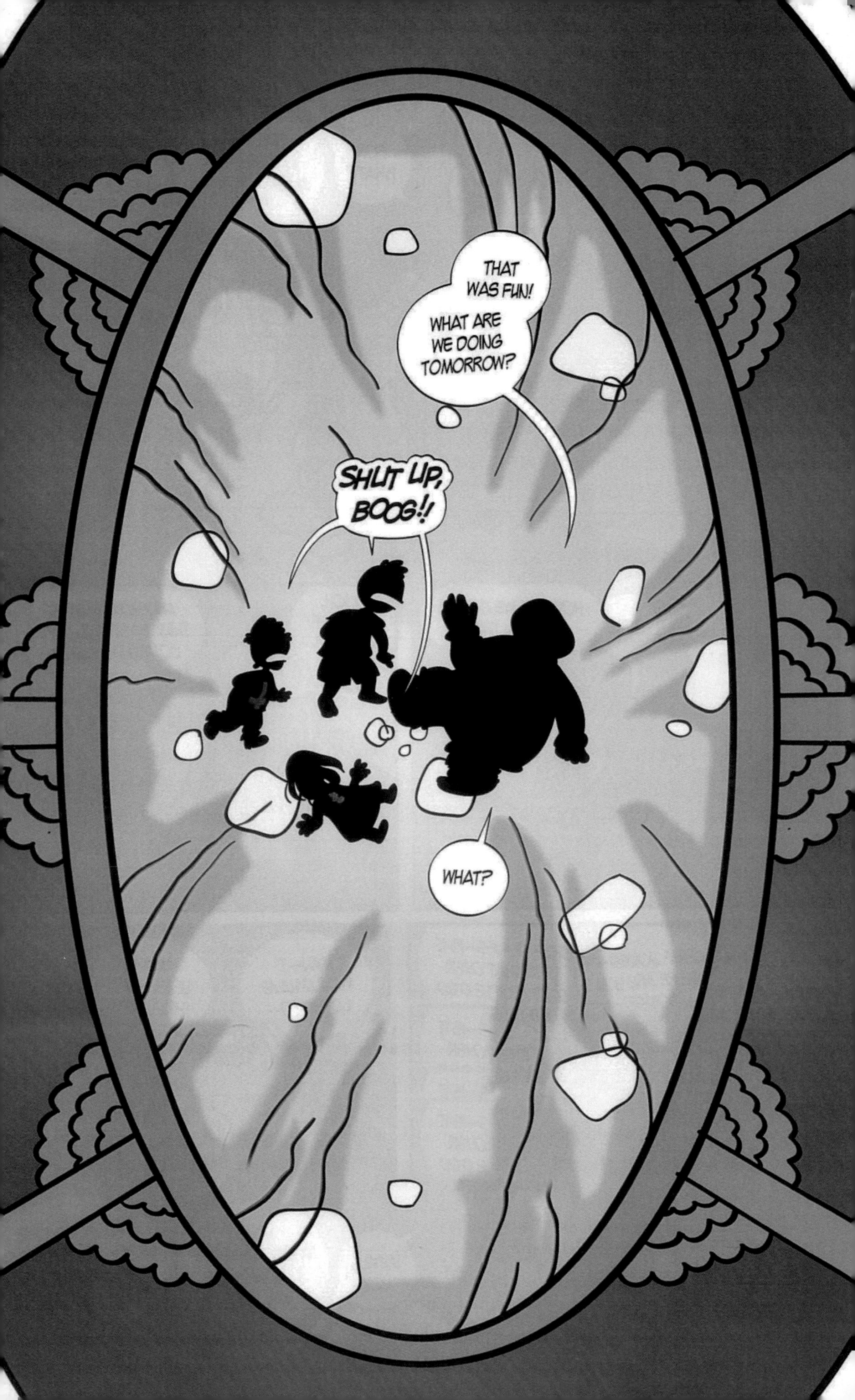
THAT WAS FUN!
WHAT ARE WE DOING TOMORROW?
SHUT UP, BOOG!!
WHAT?

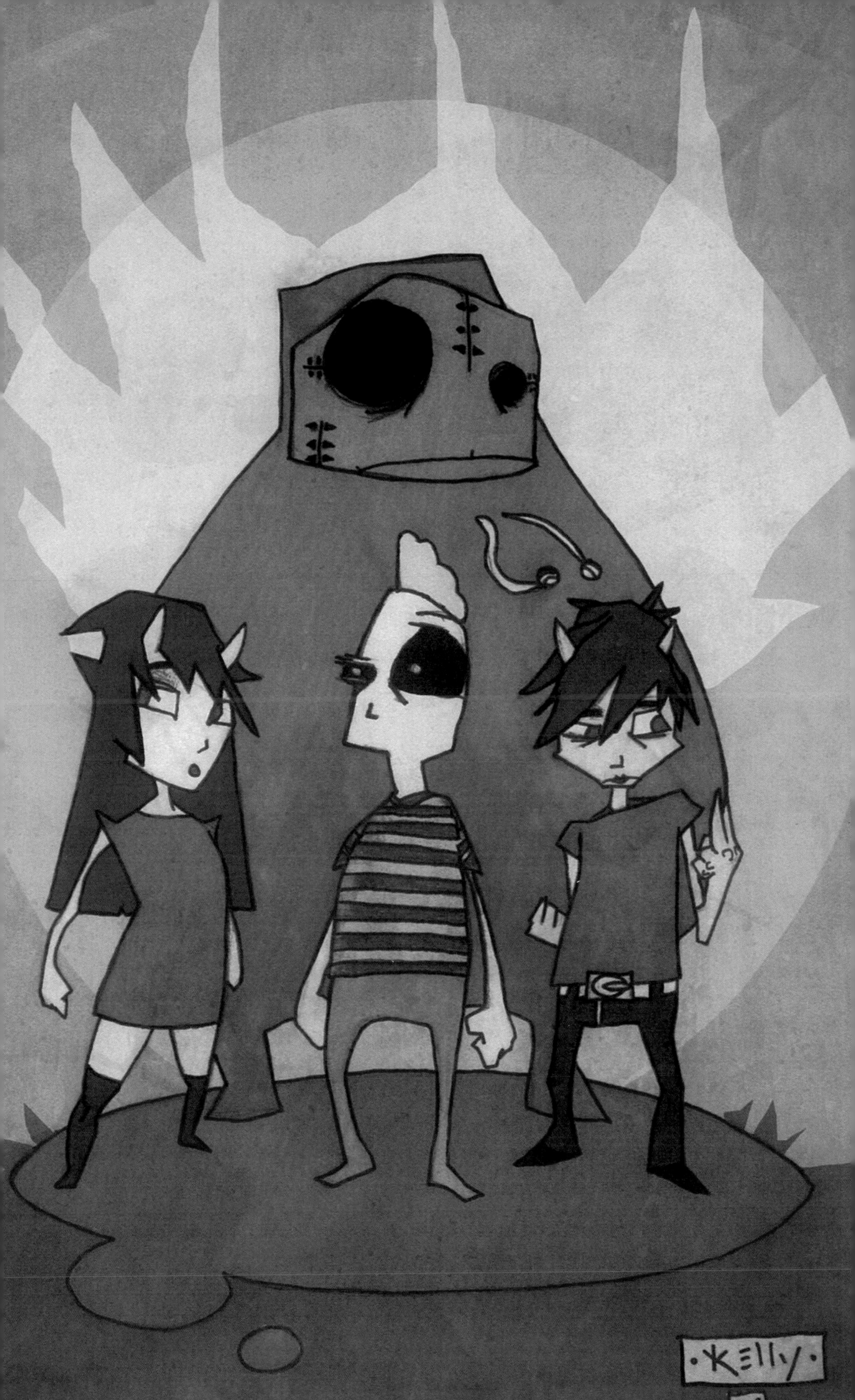
·Kelly·

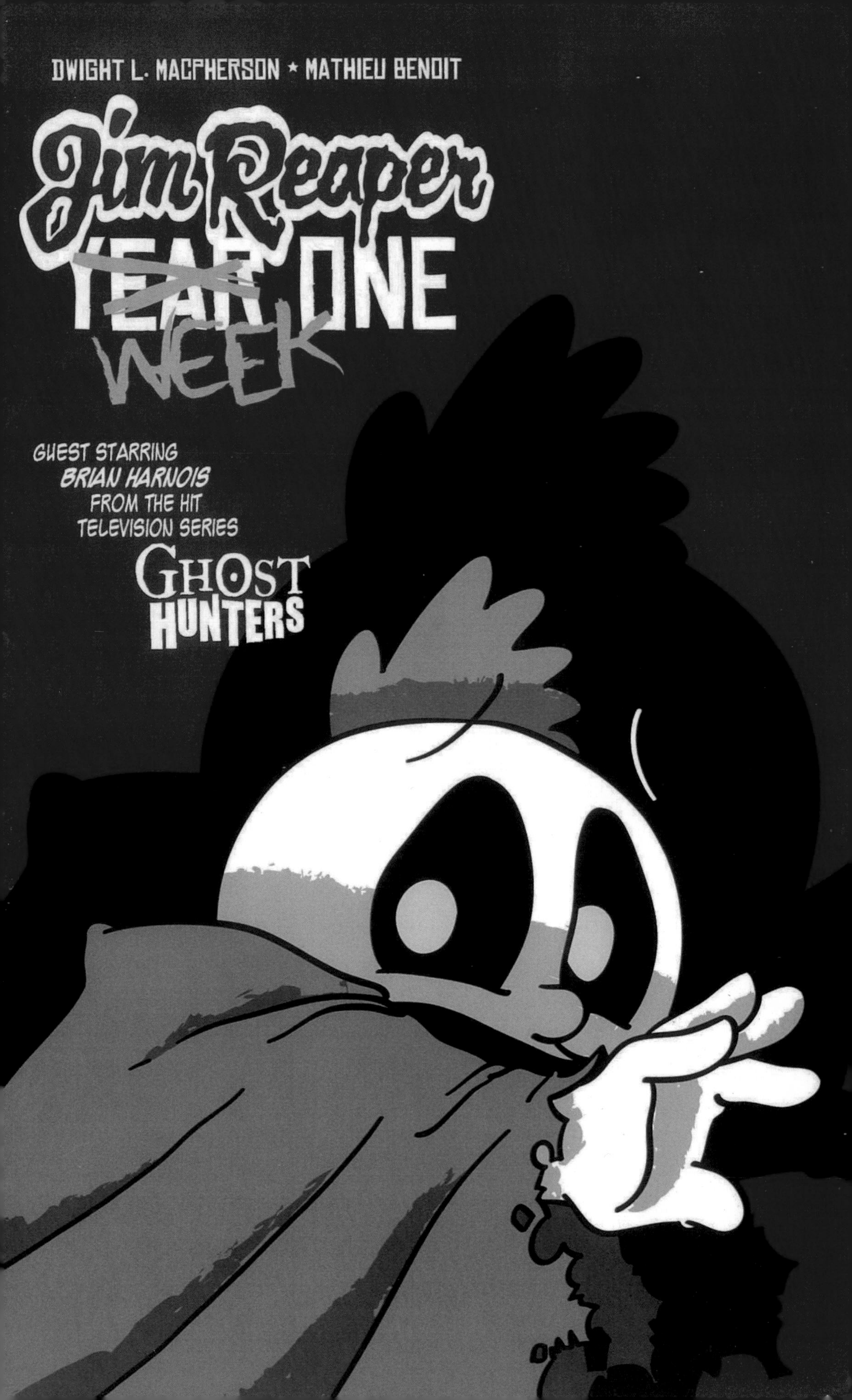
DWIGHT L. MACPHERSON ★ MATHIEU BENOIT
Jim Reaper
YEAR ONE
WEEK
GUEST STARRING
BRIAN HARNOIS
FROM THE HIT
TELEVISION SERIES
GHOST
HUNTERS

Jim Reaper
~~Year~~ Week One

BONUS CONTENT

Created and Written by:
Dwight L. MacPherson

Art by:
Mathieu Benoit, JORZAC, and Eric Morin

Colors by:
Michael Wulf and Andy Jewett

Letters by:
Mathieu Benoit and Thomas Mauer

Production Assistance by:
Thomas Mauer

Guest Starring:
Brian Harnois
from the hit Television Series GHOST HUNTERS

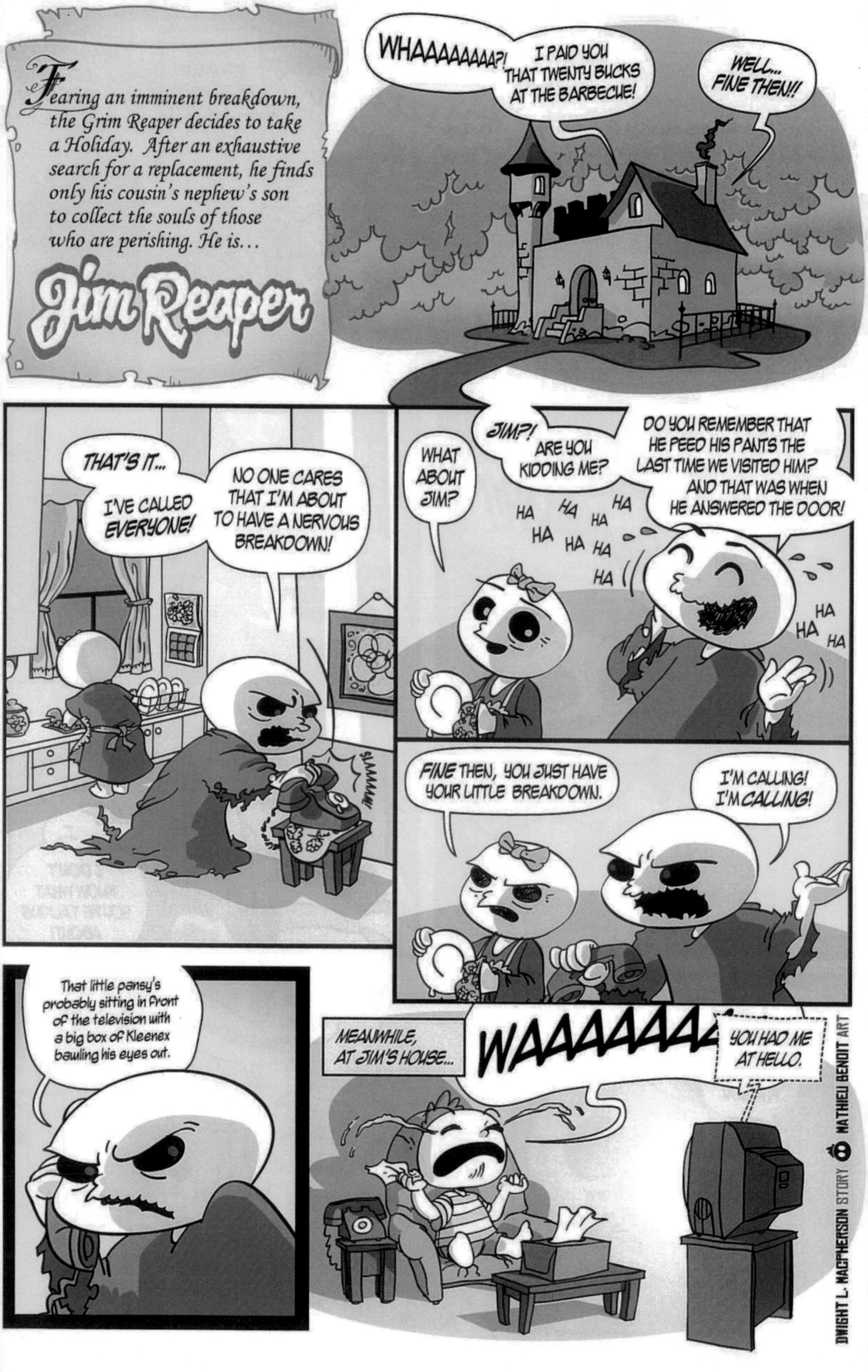
Fearing an imminent breakdown, the Grim Reaper decides to take a Holiday. After an exhaustive search for a replacement, he finds only his cousin's nephew's son to collect the souls of those who are perishing. He is…
Jim Reaper
WHAAAAAAAA?!
I PAID YOU THAT TWENTY BUCKS AT THE BARBECUE!
WELL... FINE THEN!!
THAT'S IT... I'VE CALLED EVERYONE!
NO ONE CARES THAT I'M ABOUT TO HAVE A NERVOUS BREAKDOWN!
SLAAAAAM!
WHAT ABOUT JIM?
JIM?! ARE YOU KIDDING ME?
DO YOU REMEMBER THAT HE PEED HIS PANTS THE LAST TIME WE VISITED HIM? AND THAT WAS WHEN HE ANSWERED THE DOOR!
HA HA HA HA HA HA HA HA HA
HA HA HA
FINE THEN, YOU JUST HAVE YOUR LITTLE BREAKDOWN.
I'M CALLING! I'M CALLING!
That little pansy's probably sitting in front of the television with a big box of Kleenex bawling his eyes out.
MEANWHILE, AT JIM'S HOUSE...
WAAAAAAA
YOU HAD ME AT HELLO.
DWIGHT L. MACPHERSON STORY MATHIEU BENOIT ART

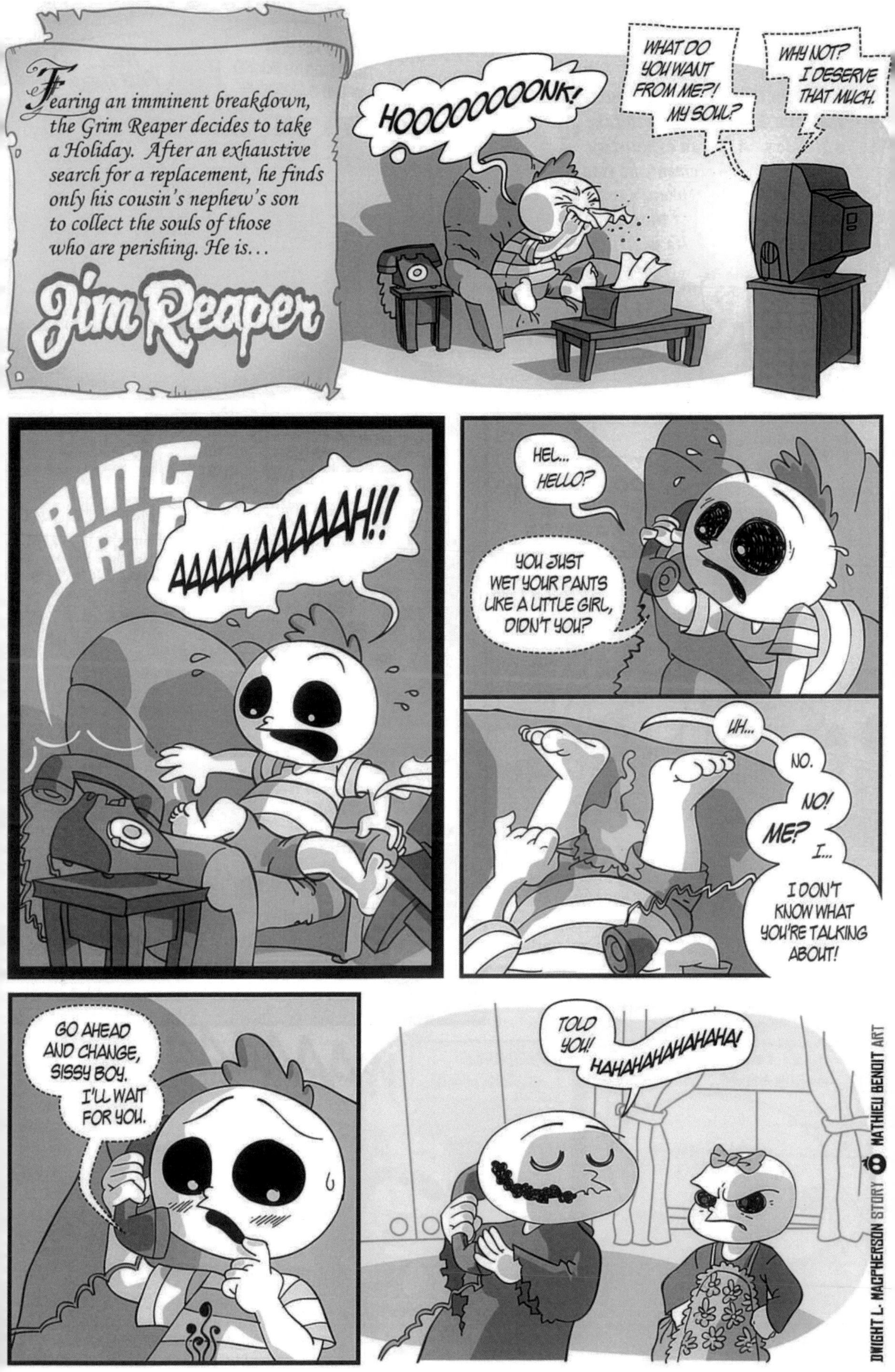

Fearing an imminent breakdown, the Grim Reaper decides to take a Holiday. After an exhaustive search for a replacement, he finds only his cousin's nephew's son to collect the souls of those who are perishing. He is...
Jim Reaper
HOOOOOOOONK!
WHAT DO YOU WANT FROM ME?! MY SOUL?
WHY NOT? I DESERVE THAT MUCH.
AAAAAAAAAAH!!
HEL... HELLO?
YOU JUST WET YOUR PANTS LIKE A LITTLE GIRL, DIDN'T YOU?
UH...
NO.
NO!
ME?
I...
I DON'T KNOW WHAT YOU'RE TALKING ABOUT!
GO AHEAD AND CHANGE, SISSY BOY. I'LL WAIT FOR YOU.
TOLD YOU!
HAHAHAHAHAHAHA!

DWIGHT L. MACPHERSON STORY · MATHIEU BENOIT ART

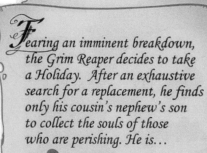

Fearing an imminent breakdown, the Grim Reaper decides to take a Holiday. After an exhaustive search for a replacement, he finds only his cousin's nephew's son to collect the souls of those who are perishing. He is...

YOU STOP THAT THIS INSTANT! IF JIM DOESN'T DO THIS FOR YOU, YOU'RE STUCK!

OH, POO! I'M JUST HAVING SOME FUN WITH THE LITTLE TWIT!

WHERE'S THE HARM IN THAT?

HA HA HA HA HA HA HA HA HA HA HA HA HA HA

HA HA HA HA HA HA HA HA HA HA HA

DON'T PAY YOUR UNCLE GRIM ANY MIND, SON. GO AHEAD AND CLEAN UP. WE'LL COME INSIDE AND WAIT.

LATER...

AH, NO HARD FEELINGS THERE, JIMMY! AND JUST TO PROVE IT TO YOU...

BOOGA BOOGA!

AAAAAAH!

WHAT'S THAT AWFUL SMELL? JIM?!

DWIGHT L. MACPHERSON STORY ● MATHIEU BENOIT ART

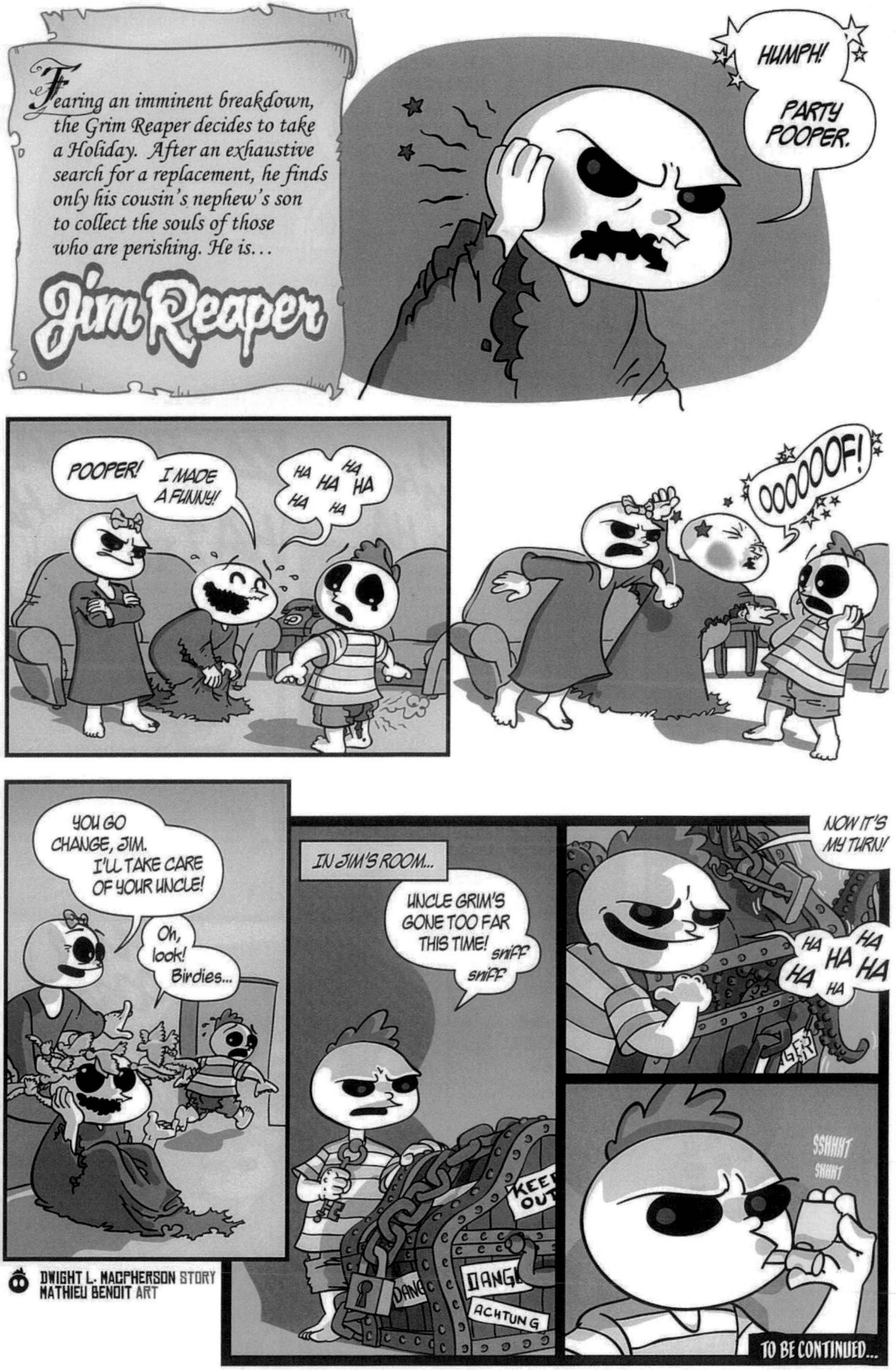
Fearing an imminent breakdown, the Grim Reaper decides to take a Holiday. After an exhaustive search for a replacement, he finds only his cousin's nephew's son to collect the souls of those who are perishing. He is…
Jim Reaper
HUMPH!
PARTY POOPER.
POOPER!
I MADE A FUNNY!
HA HA HA HA HA HA
OOOOOOF!
YOU GO CHANGE, JIM. I'LL TAKE CARE OF YOUR UNCLE!
Oh, look! Birdies...
IN JIM'S ROOM...
UNCLE GRIM'S GONE TOO FAR THIS TIME! sniff sniff
ACHTUNG
NOW IT'S MY TURN!
HA HA HA HA HA HA
SSHHHT SHHHT
TO BE CONTINUED...
DWIGHT L. MACPHERSON STORY
MATHIEU BENOIT ART

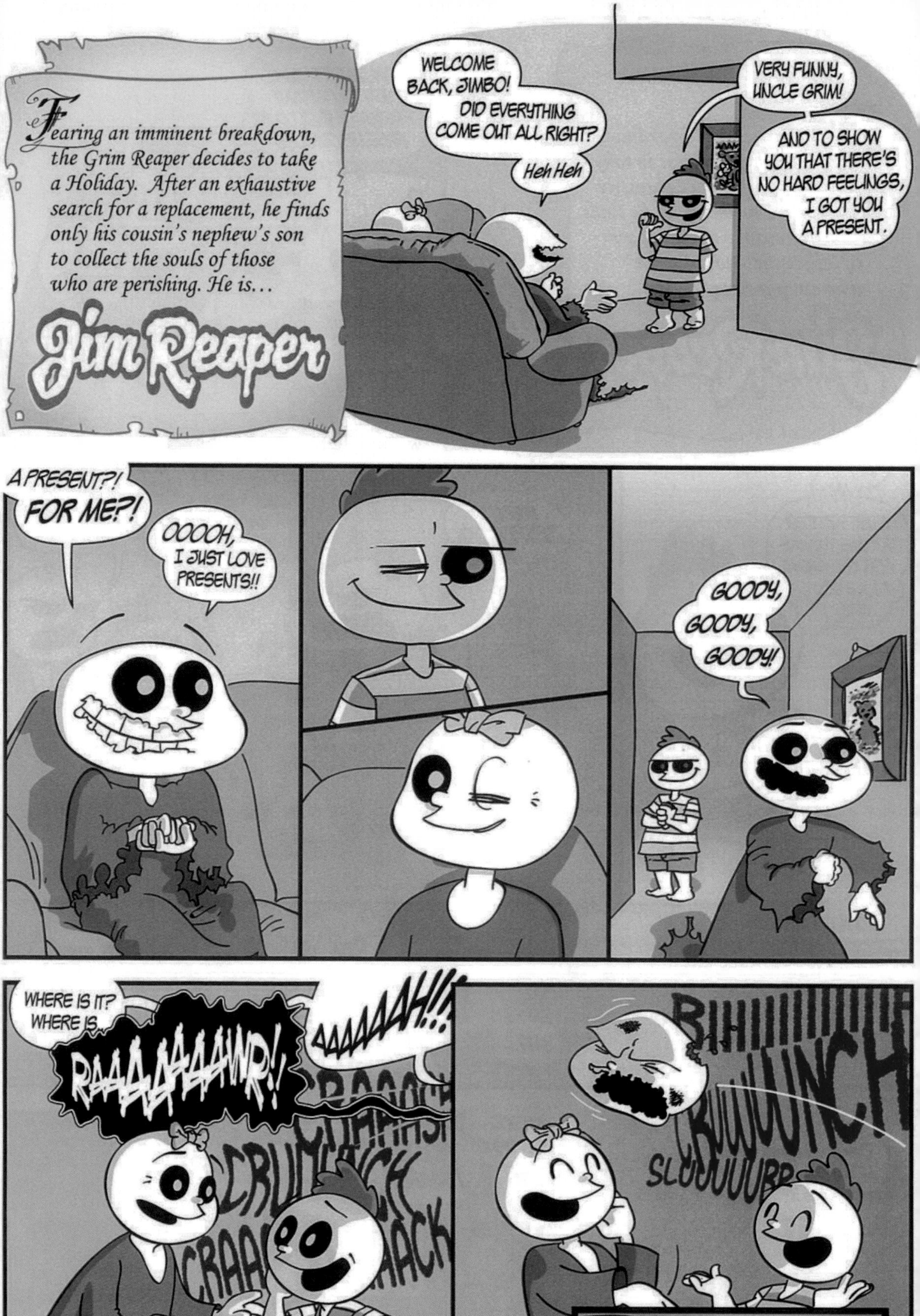

Fearing an imminent breakdown, the Grim Reaper decides to take a Holiday. After an exhaustive search for a replacement, he finds only his cousin's nephew's son to collect the souls of those who are perishing. He is…
Jim Reaper
WELCOME BACK, JIMBO!
DID EVERYTHING COME OUT ALL RIGHT?
Heh Heh
VERY FUNNY, UNCLE GRIM!
AND TO SHOW YOU THAT THERE'S NO HARD FEELINGS, I GOT YOU A PRESENT.
A PRESENT?! FOR ME?!
OOOOH, I JUST LOVE PRESENTS!!
GOODY, GOODY, GOODY!
WHERE IS IT? WHERE IS...
RAAAAAAAWR!!
AAAAAAH!!!
CRUNCH
SLUUUUURP
THAT'S THE WORST PRESENT I'VE EVER GOTTEN!!
DWIGHT L. MACPHERSON STORY
MATHIEU BENOIT ART

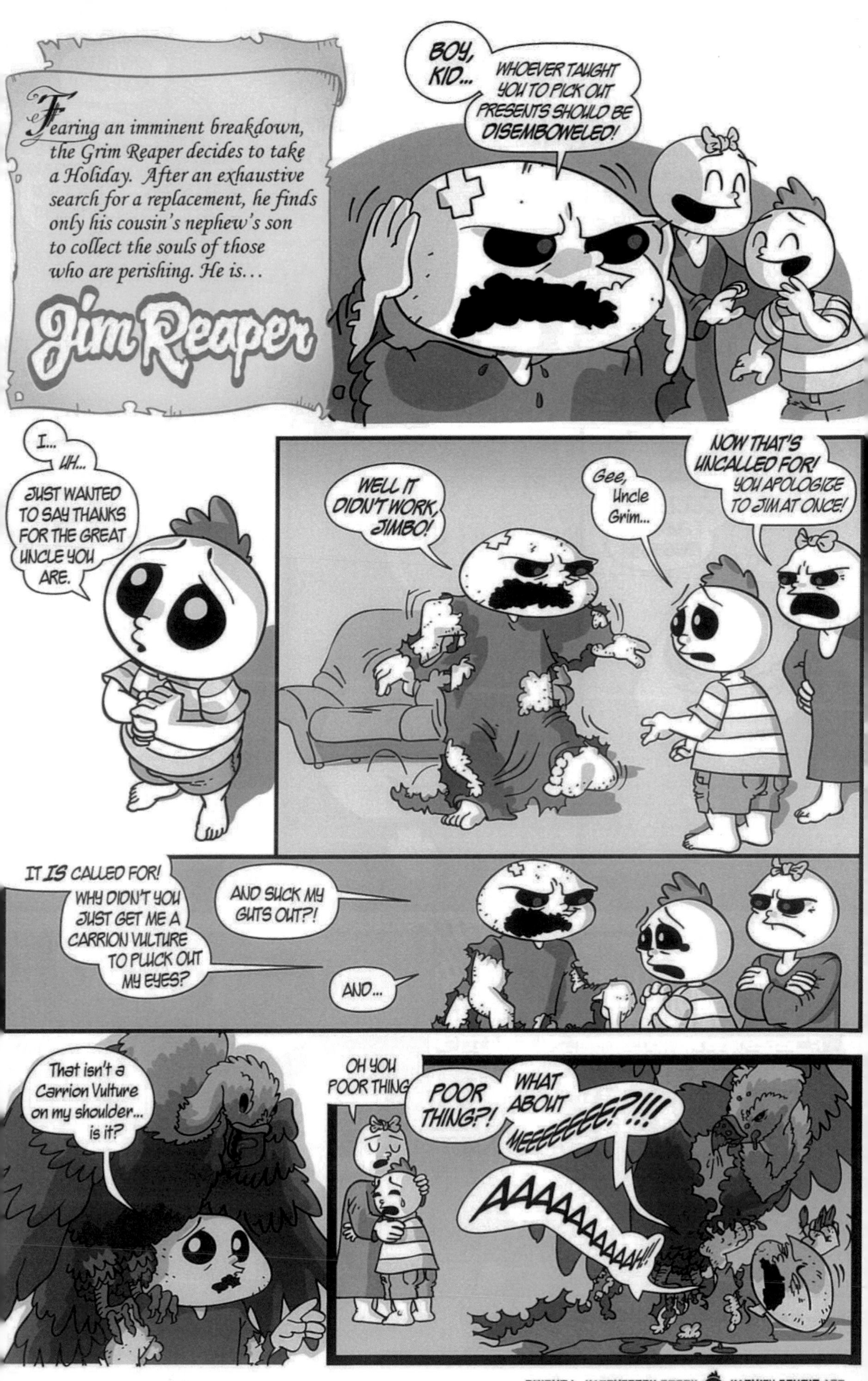
Fearing an imminent breakdown, the Grim Reaper decides to take a Holiday. After an exhaustive search for a replacement, he finds only his cousin's nephew's son to collect the souls of those who are perishing. He is…
Jim Reaper
BOY, KID…
WHOEVER TAUGHT YOU TO PICK OUT PRESENTS SHOULD BE DISEMBOWELED!
I… UH…
JUST WANTED TO SAY THANKS FOR THE GREAT UNCLE YOU ARE.
WELL IT DIDN'T WORK, JIMBO!
Gee, Uncle Grim…
NOW THAT'S UNCALLED FOR!
YOU APOLOGIZE TO JIM AT ONCE!
IT IS CALLED FOR!
WHY DIDN'T YOU JUST GET ME A CARRION VULTURE TO PLUCK OUT MY EYES?
AND SUCK MY GUTS OUT?!
AND…
That isn't a Carrion Vulture on my shoulder… is it?
OH YOU POOR THING
POOR THING?!
WHAT ABOUT MEEEEEEEE?!!!
AAAAAAAAAAH!!!

DWIGHT L. MACPHERSON STORY MATHIEU BENOIT ART

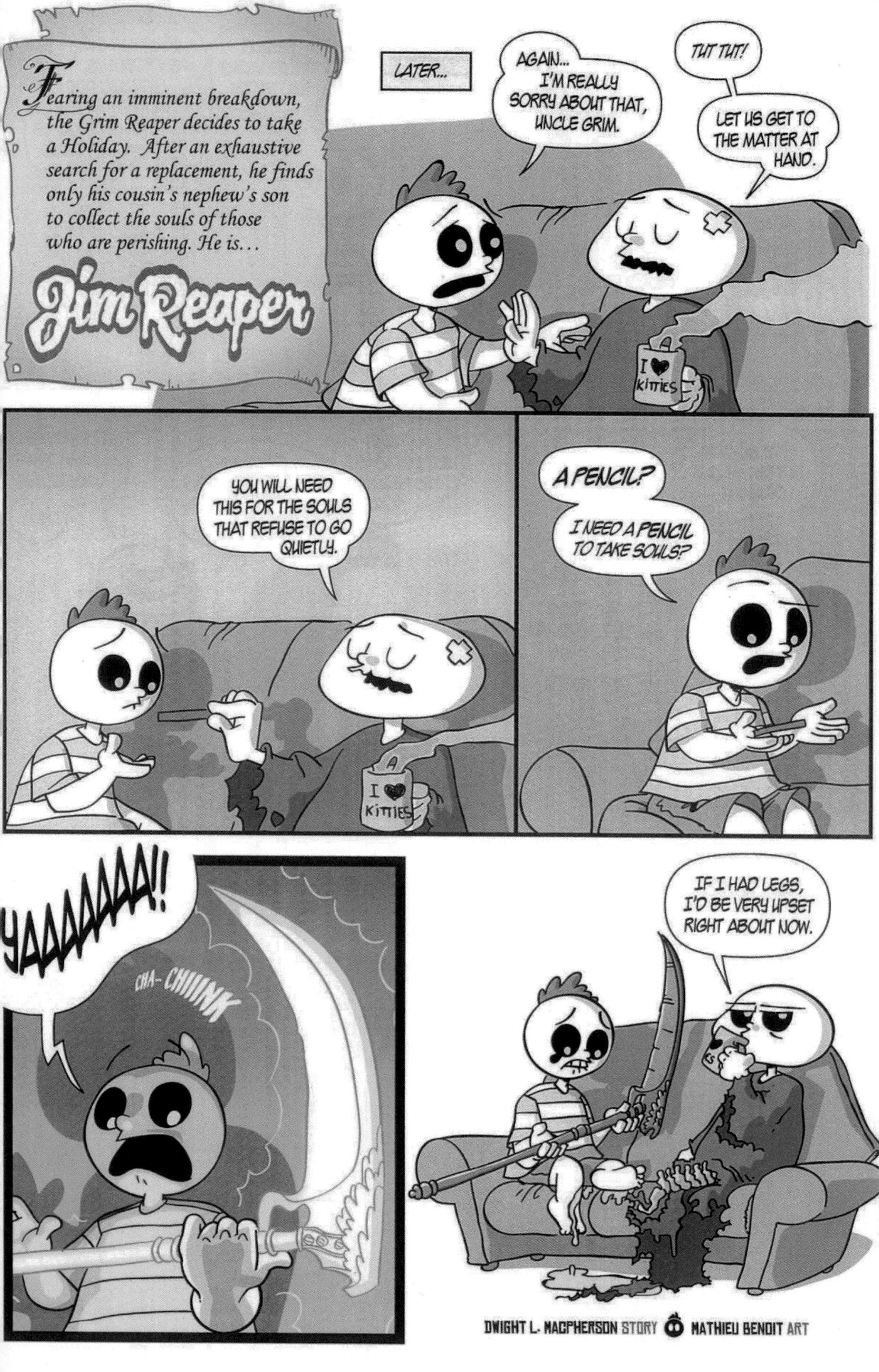
Fearing an imminent breakdown, the Grim Reaper decides to take a Holiday. After an exhaustive search for a replacement, he finds only his cousin's nephew's son to collect the souls of those who are perishing. He is...
Jim Reaper
LATER...
AGAIN... I'M REALLY SORRY ABOUT THAT, UNCLE GRIM.
TUT TUT!
LET US GET TO THE MATTER AT HAND.
I ♥ KITTIES
YOU WILL NEED THIS FOR THE SOULS THAT REFUSE TO GO QUIETLY.
A PENCIL?
I NEED A PENCIL TO TAKE SOULS?
YAAAAAAA!!
CHA-CHIIINK
IF I HAD LEGS, I'D BE VERY UPSET RIGHT ABOUT NOW.

DWIGHT L. MACPHERSON STORY MATHIEU BENOIT ART

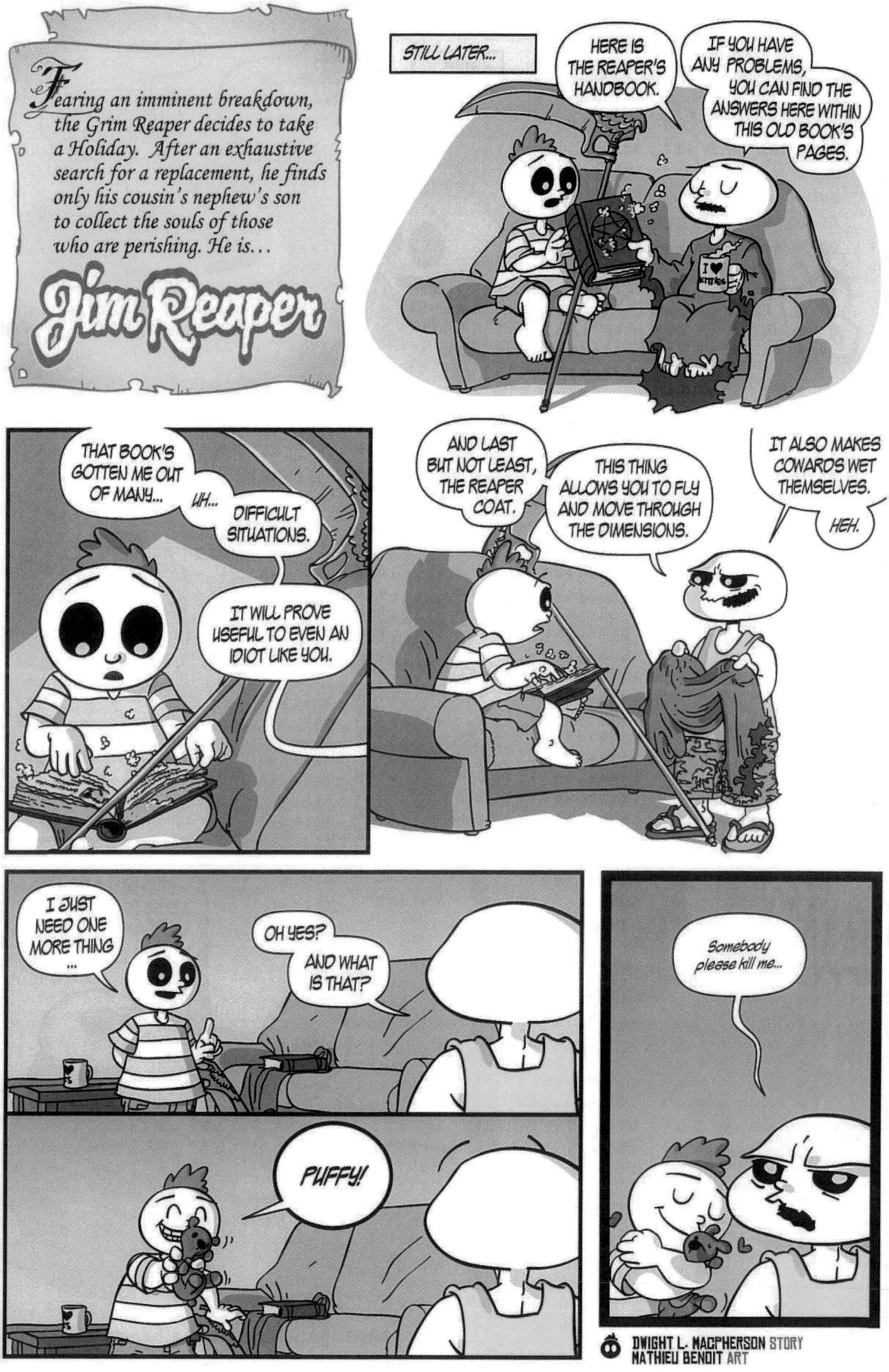
Fearing an imminent breakdown, the Grim Reaper decides to take a Holiday. After an exhaustive search for a replacement, he finds only his cousin's nephew's son to collect the souls of those who are perishing. He is...
Jim Reaper
STILL LATER...
HERE IS THE REAPER'S HANDBOOK.
IF YOU HAVE ANY PROBLEMS, YOU CAN FIND THE ANSWERS HERE WITHIN THIS OLD BOOK'S PAGES.
THAT BOOK'S GOTTEN ME OUT OF MANY...
UH...
DIFFICULT SITUATIONS.
IT WILL PROVE USEFUL TO EVEN AN IDIOT LIKE YOU.
AND LAST BUT NOT LEAST, THE REAPER COAT.
THIS THING ALLOWS YOU TO FLY AND MOVE THROUGH THE DIMENSIONS.
IT ALSO MAKES COWARDS WET THEMSELVES.
HEH.
I JUST NEED ONE MORE THING ...
OH YES?
AND WHAT IS THAT?
PUFFY!
Somebody please kill me...

DWIGHT L. MACPHERSON STORY
MATHIEU BENOIT ART

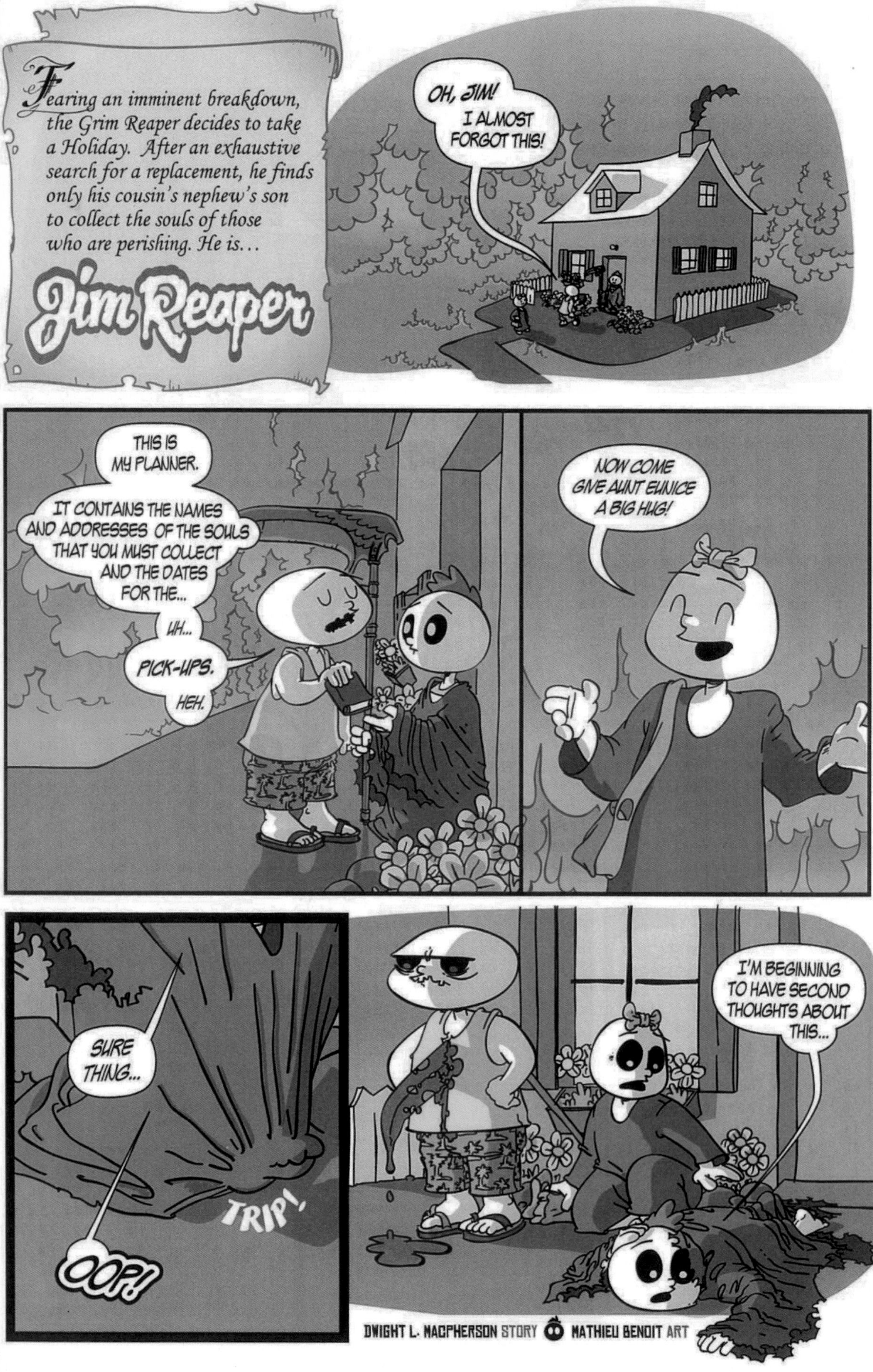
Fearing an imminent breakdown, the Grim Reaper decides to take a Holiday. After an exhaustive search for a replacement, he finds only his cousin's nephew's son to collect the souls of those who are perishing. He is...
Jim Reaper
OH, JIM! I ALMOST FORGOT THIS!
THIS IS MY PLANNER.
IT CONTAINS THE NAMES AND ADDRESSES OF THE SOULS THAT YOU MUST COLLECT AND THE DATES FOR THE...
UH...
PICK-UPS.
HEH.
NOW COME GIVE AUNT EUNICE A BIG HUG!
SURE THING...
TRIP!
OOP!
I'M BEGINNING TO HAVE SECOND THOUGHTS ABOUT THIS...
DWIGHT L. MACPHERSON STORY MATHIEU BENOIT ART

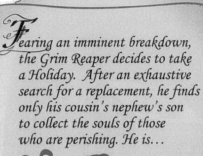

*F*earing an imminent breakdown, the Grim Reaper decides to take a Holiday. After an exhaustive search for a replacement, he finds only his cousin's nephew's son to collect the souls of those who are perishing. He is...

Jim Reaper

GOODBYE, JIM!

SO LONG, JIMBO...

HA HA HA HA HA HA HA HA HA HA HA HA HA HA HA HA

...BEEN NICE KNOWING YOU!

SMAAACK

OUCH!

WELL, PUFFY... WHAT SHOULD WE DO FIRST?

BUT THAT'S ILLEGAL IN 14 STATES!

DWIGHT L. MACPHERSON STORY
MATHIEU BENOIT ART

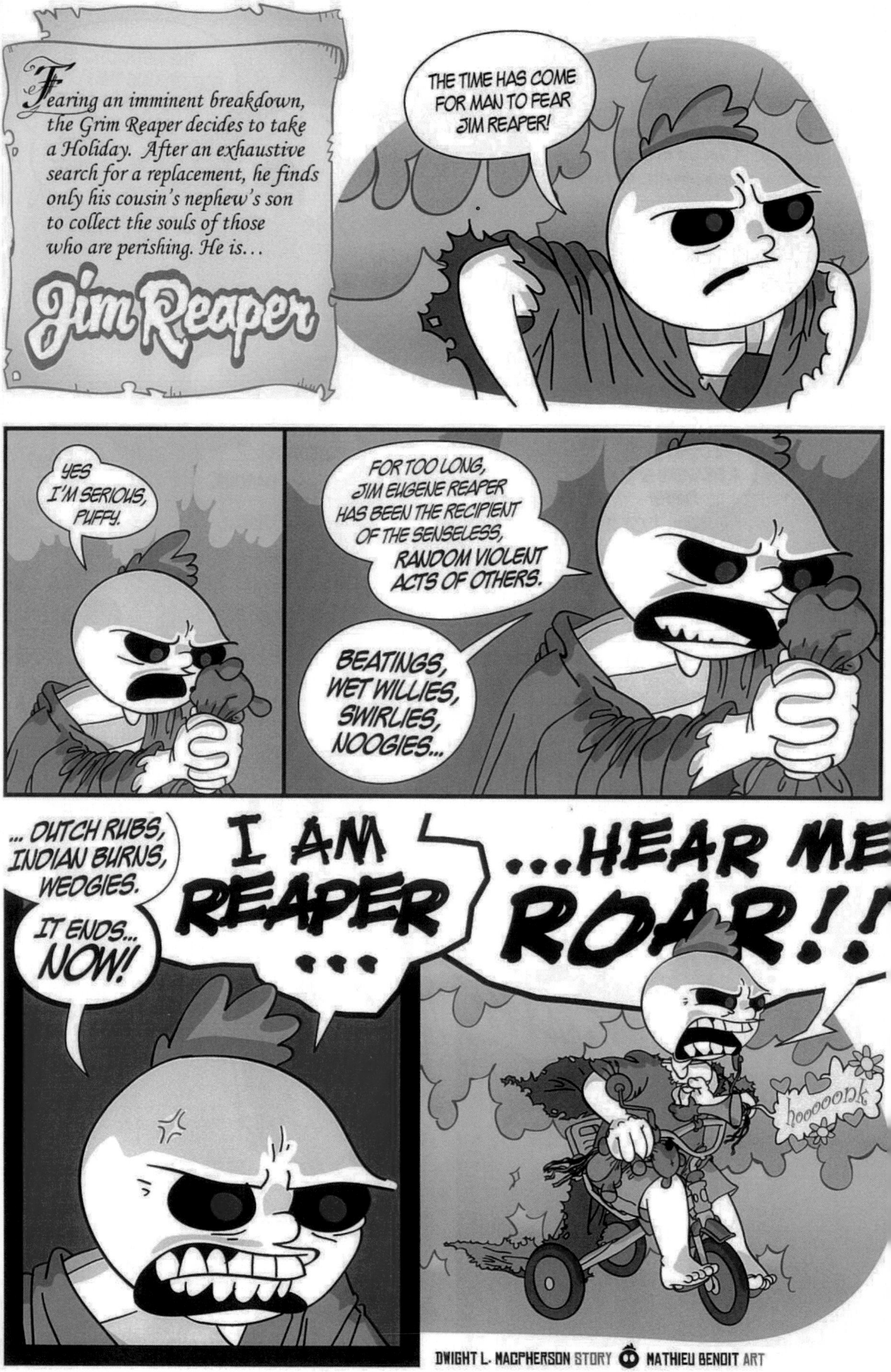
Fearing an imminent breakdown, the Grim Reaper decides to take a Holiday. After an exhaustive search for a replacement, he finds only his cousin's nephew's son to collect the souls of those who are perishing. He is…
Jim Reaper
THE TIME HAS COME FOR MAN TO FEAR JIM REAPER!
YES I'M SERIOUS, PUFFY.
FOR TOO LONG, JIM EUGENE REAPER HAS BEEN THE RECIPIENT OF THE SENSELESS, RANDOM VIOLENT ACTS OF OTHERS.
BEATINGS, WET WILLIES, SWIRLIES, NOOGIES...
... DUTCH RUBS, INDIAN BURNS, WEDGIES.
IT ENDS... NOW!
I AM REAPER ...
...HEAR ME ROAR!!
hoooooonk

DWIGHT L. MACPHERSON STORY · MATHIEU BENOIT ART

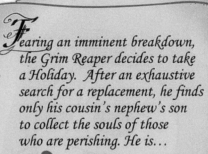

Fearing an imminent breakdown, the Grim Reaper decides to take a Holiday. After an exhaustive search for a replacement, he finds only his cousin's nephew's son to collect the souls of those who are perishing. He is…
Jim Reaper
OKAY, PUFFY...
THE INSTRUCTIONS FOR OPENING THE PORTAL HAVE TO BE IN HERE SOMEWHERE, SO BE PATIENT.
I DON'T NEED A BRAVERY SPELL, PUFFY!
I TOLD YOU...
I AM A CHANGED REAPER!
FOUND IT!
OKAY, HERE GOES NOTHING ...
PATEFACIO.
BAROUS.
PRODIGIUM.
PATEFACIO BAROUS PRODIGIUM!
WHAT'CHOO WANT?!
AAAAAAH!
WHAT'D I SAY?
DWIGHT L. MACPHERSON STORY
MATHIEU BENOIT ART

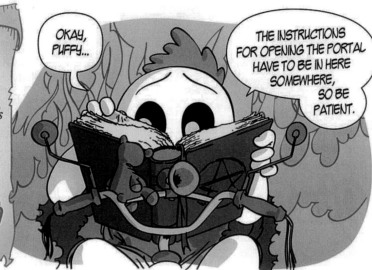

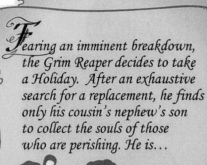

Fearing an imminent breakdown, the Grim Reaper decides to take a Holiday. After an exhaustive search for a replacement, he finds only his cousin's nephew's son to collect the souls of those who are perishing. He is...

Jim Reaper

Ooooooh...

YOU OKAY, KID?

YOU AIN'T THE GRIM REAPER, BOY!

WHAT'CHOO DOIN' TRYING TO OPEN THE PORTAL ANYWAY?

UH... YOU ALMOST SCARED ME THERE, PORTAL!

I... UH...

WASN'T EXPECTING YOU TO BE A TALKING PORTAL.

ALMOST SCARED YOU?! HAHAHAHAHA

BOY, YOU JUST @?*!%$ YOUR DRAWERS!

HA HA HA HA HA HA HA

NO I DIDN'T!

NOT THIS TIME!

NOT THIS TIME?! HAHAHAHAHAHA

OH... HAHA... IT HURTS! HA HA HA HA HA HA HA HA

DWIGHT L. MACPHERSON STORY ● MATHIEU BENOIT ART

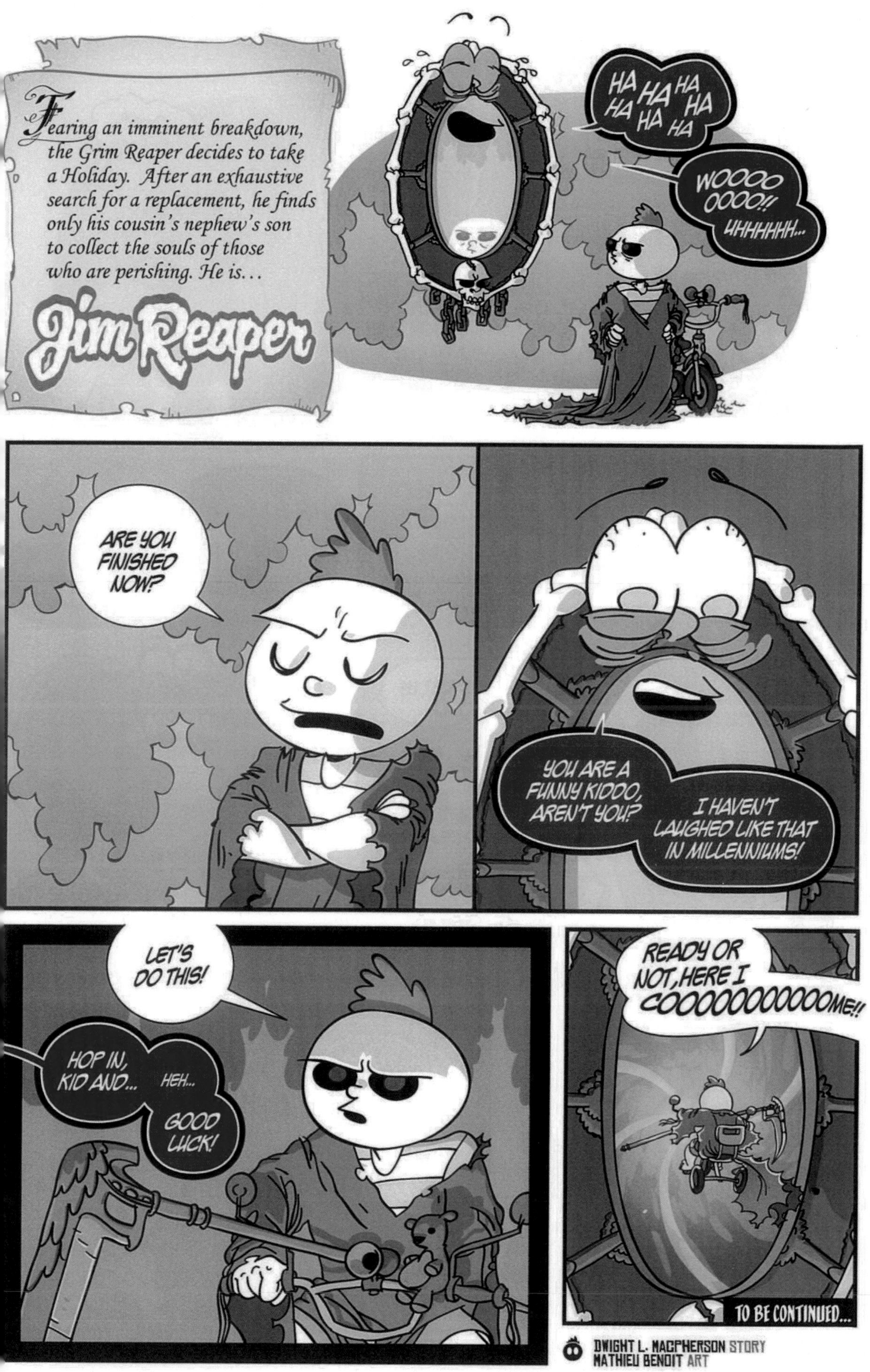
Fearing an imminent breakdown, the Grim Reaper decides to take a Holiday. After an exhaustive search for a replacement, he finds only his cousin's nephew's son to collect the souls of those who are perishing. He is...
Jim Reaper
HA HA HA HA HA HA HA HA
WOOOO OOOO!! UHHHHHH...
ARE YOU FINISHED NOW?
YOU ARE A FUNNY KIDDO, AREN'T YOU?
I HAVEN'T LAUGHED LIKE THAT IN MILLENNIUMS!
LET'S DO THIS!
HOP IN, KID AND...
HEH...
GOOD LUCK!
READY OR NOT, HERE I COOOOOOOOOOOME!!
TO BE CONTINUED...
DWIGHT L. MACPHERSON STORY
MATHIEU BENOIT ART

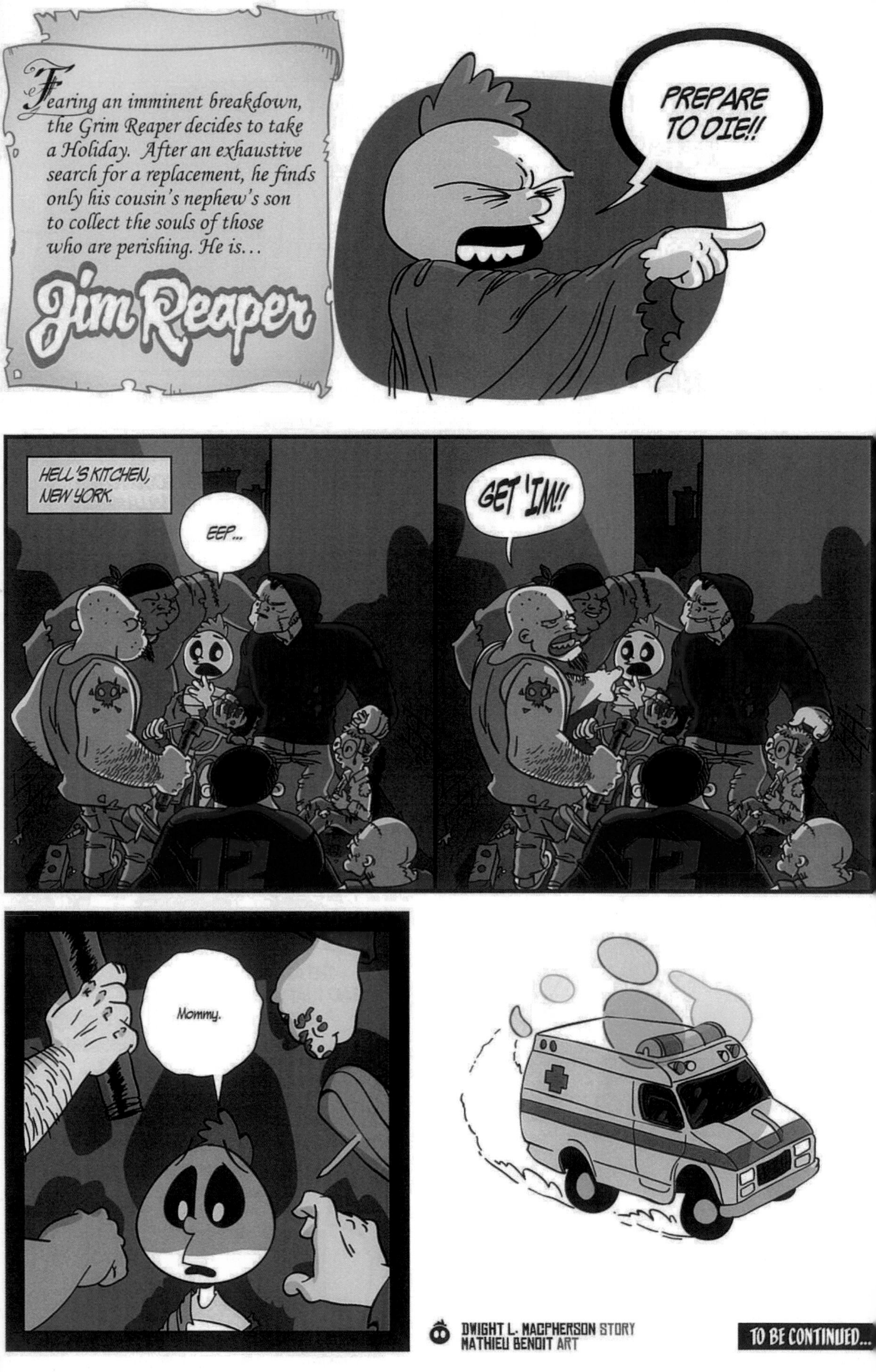

Fearing an imminent breakdown, the Grim Reaper decides to take a Holiday. After an exhaustive search for a replacement, he finds only his cousin's nephew's son to collect the souls of those who are perishing. He is…
Jim Reaper
PREPARE TO DIE!!
HELL'S KITCHEN, NEW YORK.
EEP...
GET 'IM!!
Mommy.
DWIGHT L. MACPHERSON STORY
MATHIEU BENOIT ART
TO BE CONTINUED...

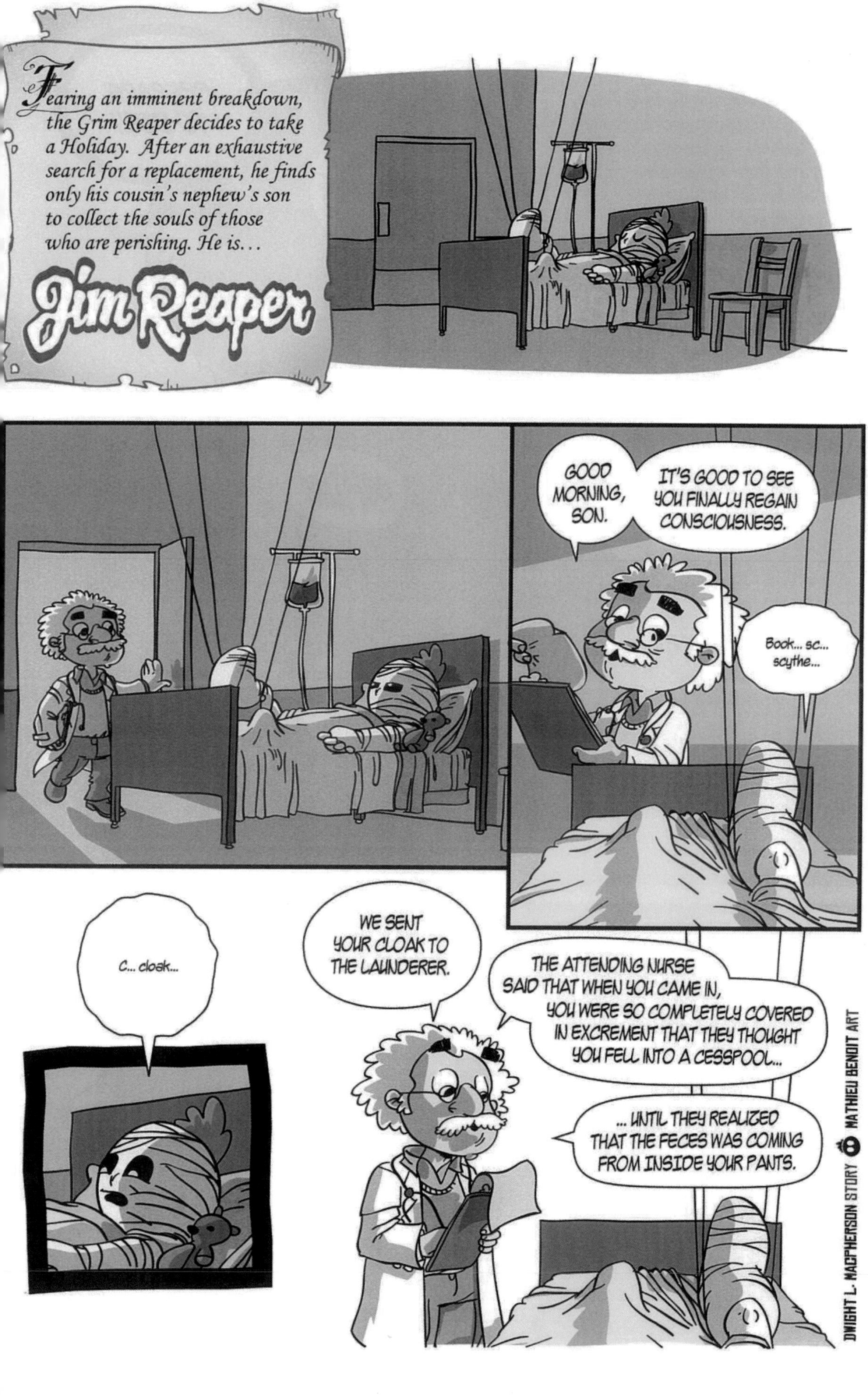
Fearing an imminent breakdown, the Grim Reaper decides to take a Holiday. After an exhaustive search for a replacement, he finds only his cousin's nephew's son to collect the souls of those who are perishing. He is…
Jim Reaper
GOOD MORNING, SON.
IT'S GOOD TO SEE YOU FINALLY REGAIN CONSCIOUSNESS.
Book… sc… scythe…
C… cloak…
WE SENT YOUR CLOAK TO THE LAUNDERER.
THE ATTENDING NURSE SAID THAT WHEN YOU CAME IN, YOU WERE SO COMPLETELY COVERED IN EXCREMENT THAT THEY THOUGHT YOU FELL INTO A CESSPOOL…
… UNTIL THEY REALIZED THAT THE FECES WAS COMING FROM INSIDE YOUR PANTS.
DWIGHT L. MACPHERSON STORY MATHIEU BENOIT ART

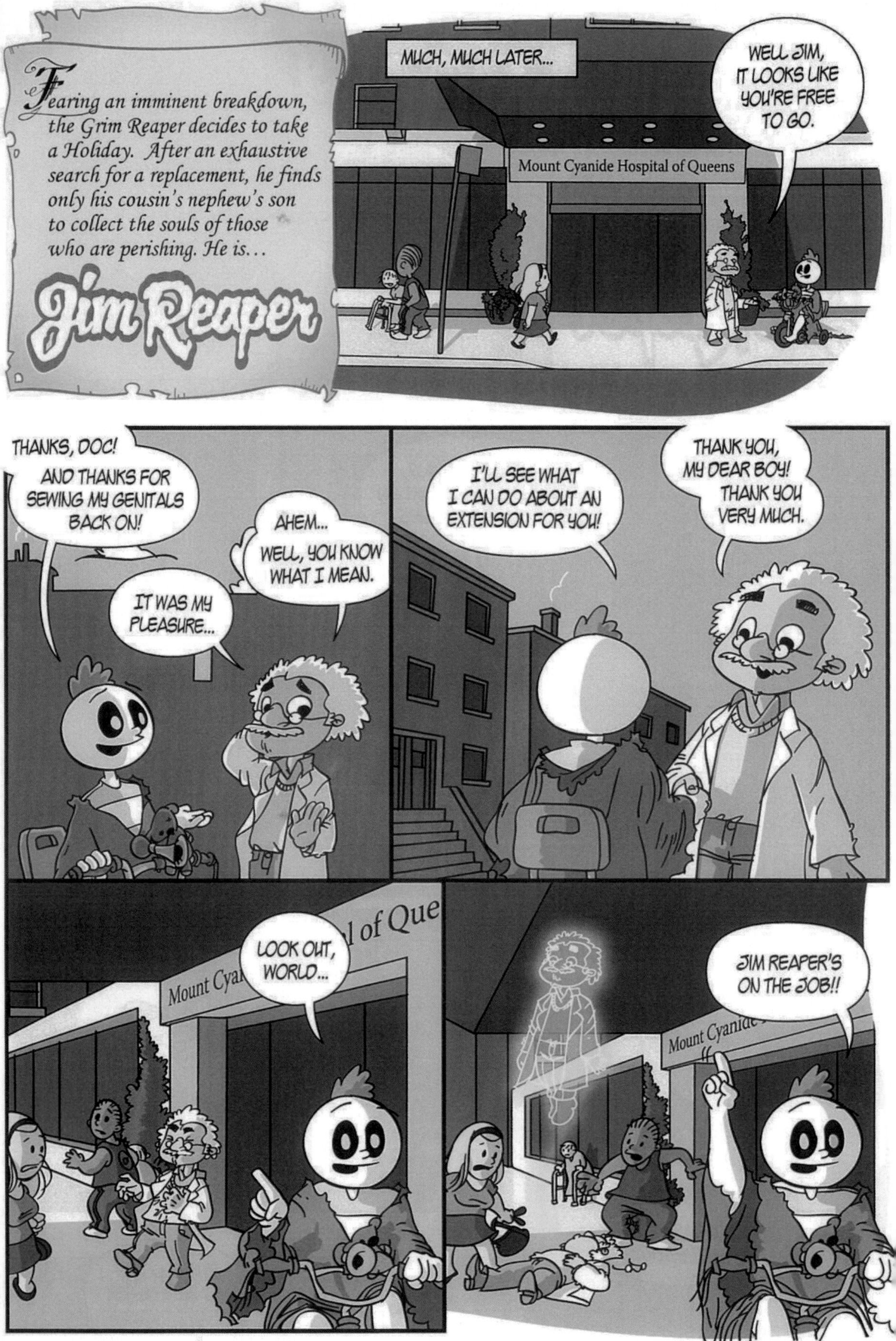
Fearing an imminent breakdown, the Grim Reaper decides to take a Holiday. After an exhaustive search for a replacement, he finds only his cousin's nephew's son to collect the souls of those who are perishing. He is…
Jim Reaper
MUCH, MUCH LATER...
Mount Cyanide Hospital of Queens
WELL JIM, IT LOOKS LIKE YOU'RE FREE TO GO.
THANKS, DOC!
AND THANKS FOR SEWING MY GENITALS BACK ON!
IT WAS MY PLEASURE...
AHEM... WELL, YOU KNOW WHAT I MEAN.
I'LL SEE WHAT I CAN DO ABOUT AN EXTENSION FOR YOU!
THANK YOU, MY DEAR BOY! THANK YOU VERY MUCH.
LOOK OUT, WORLD...
JIM REAPER'S ON THE JOB!!

DWIGHT L. MACPHERSON STORY MATHIEU BENOIT ART

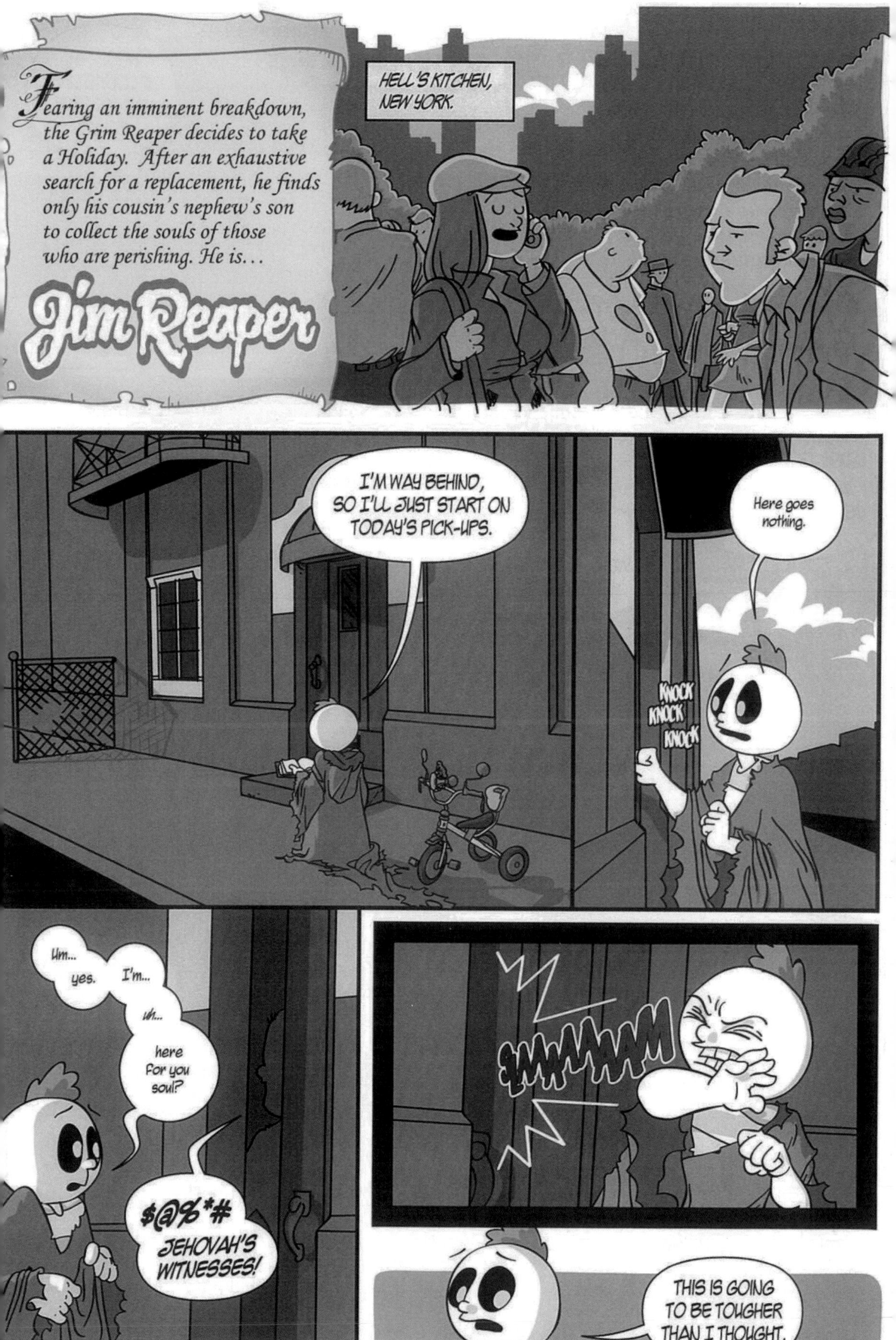
Fearing an imminent breakdown, the Grim Reaper decides to take a Holiday. After an exhaustive search for a replacement, he finds only his cousin's nephew's son to collect the souls of those who are perishing. He is...
Jim Reaper
HELL'S KITCHEN, NEW YORK.
I'M WAY BEHIND, SO I'LL JUST START ON TODAY'S PICK-UPS.
Here goes nothing.
KNOCK KNOCK KNOCK
Um... yes. I'm... uh... here for you soul?
$@%*# JEHOVAH'S WITNESSES!
SLAAAAAAM
THIS IS GOING TO BE TOUGHER THAN I THOUGHT.

WIGHT L. MACPHERSON STORY MATHIEU BENOIT ART

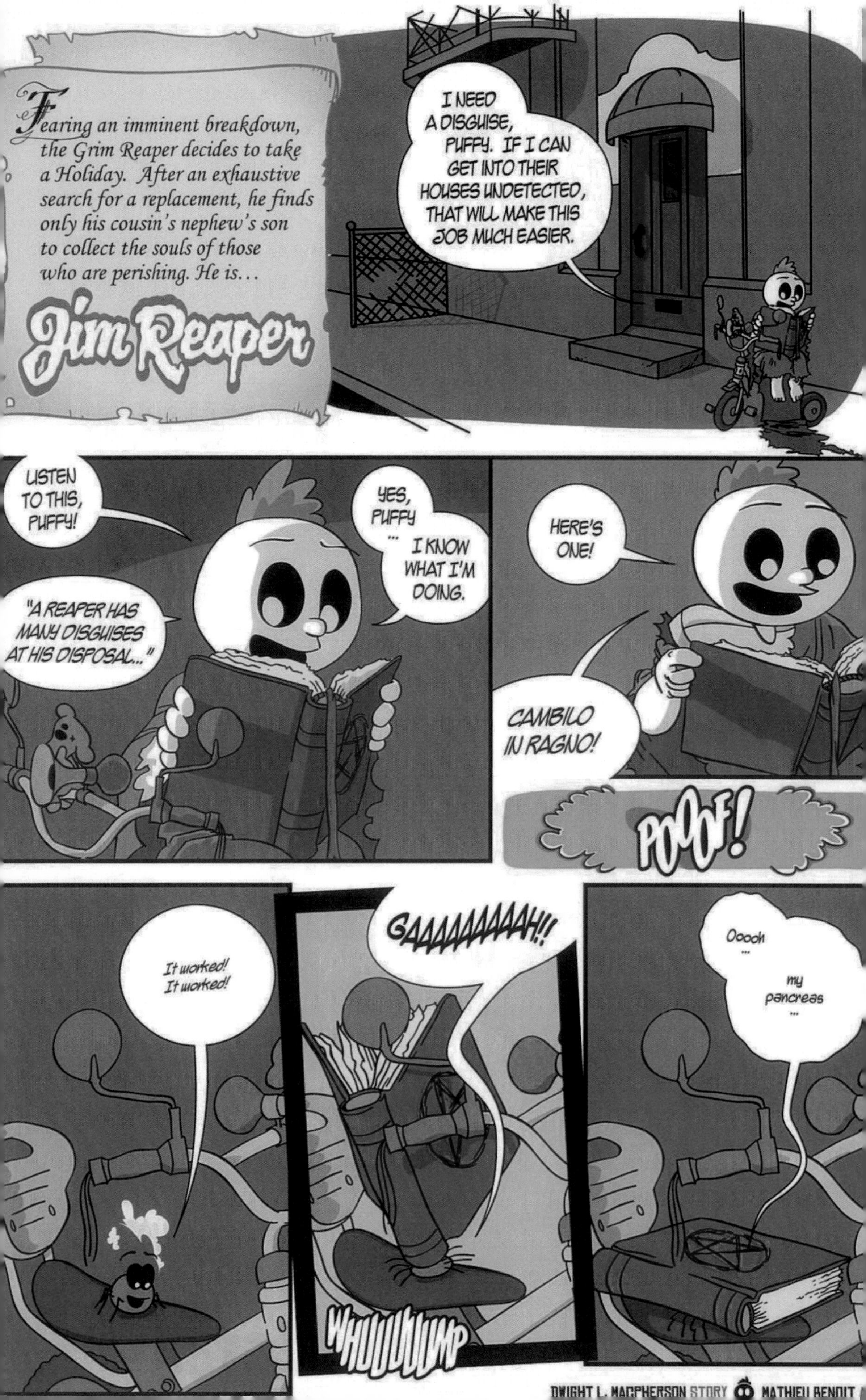
Fearing an imminent breakdown, the Grim Reaper decides to take a Holiday. After an exhaustive search for a replacement, he finds only his cousin's nephew's son to collect the souls of those who are perishing. He is…
Jim Reaper
I NEED A DISGUISE, PUFFY. IF I CAN GET INTO THEIR HOUSES UNDETECTED, THAT WILL MAKE THIS JOB MUCH EASIER.
LISTEN TO THIS, PUFFY!
"A REAPER HAS MANY DISGUISES AT HIS DISPOSAL..."
YES, PUFFY ... I KNOW WHAT I'M DOING.
HERE'S ONE!
CAMBILO IN RAGNO!
POOOF!
It worked! It worked!
GAAAAAAAAAH!!
WHUUUUUMP
Ooooh ... my pancreas ...
DWIGHT L. MACPHERSON STORY MATHIEU BENOIT

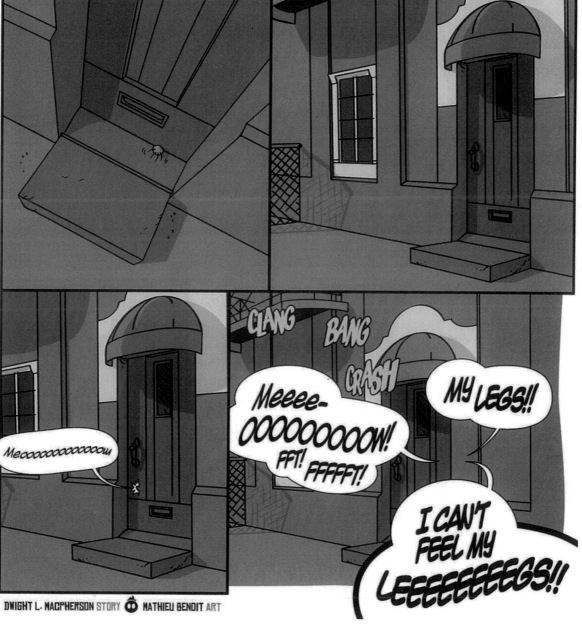

DWIGHT L. MACPHERSON STORY   MATHIEU BENOIT ART

Fearing an imminent breakdown, the Grim Reaper decides to take a Holiday. After an exhaustive search for a replacement, he finds only his cousin's nephew's son to collect the souls of those who are perishing. He is...

Jim Reaper

OKAY, YOU ASKED FOR IT, KITTY!

PATEFACIO BARDUS PRODIGIUM!

I GOT THE FELINE, BOSS!

MEOOOOO OOOOOWR

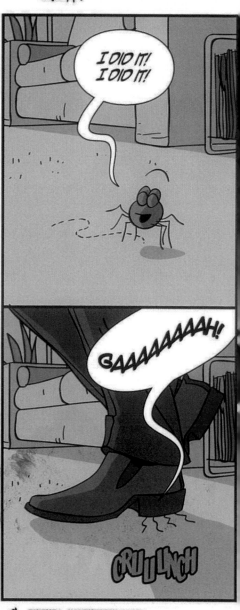

I DID IT! I DID IT!

GAAAAAAAH!

CRU U UNCH

DWIGHT L. MACPHERSON STORY
MATHIEU BENOIT ART

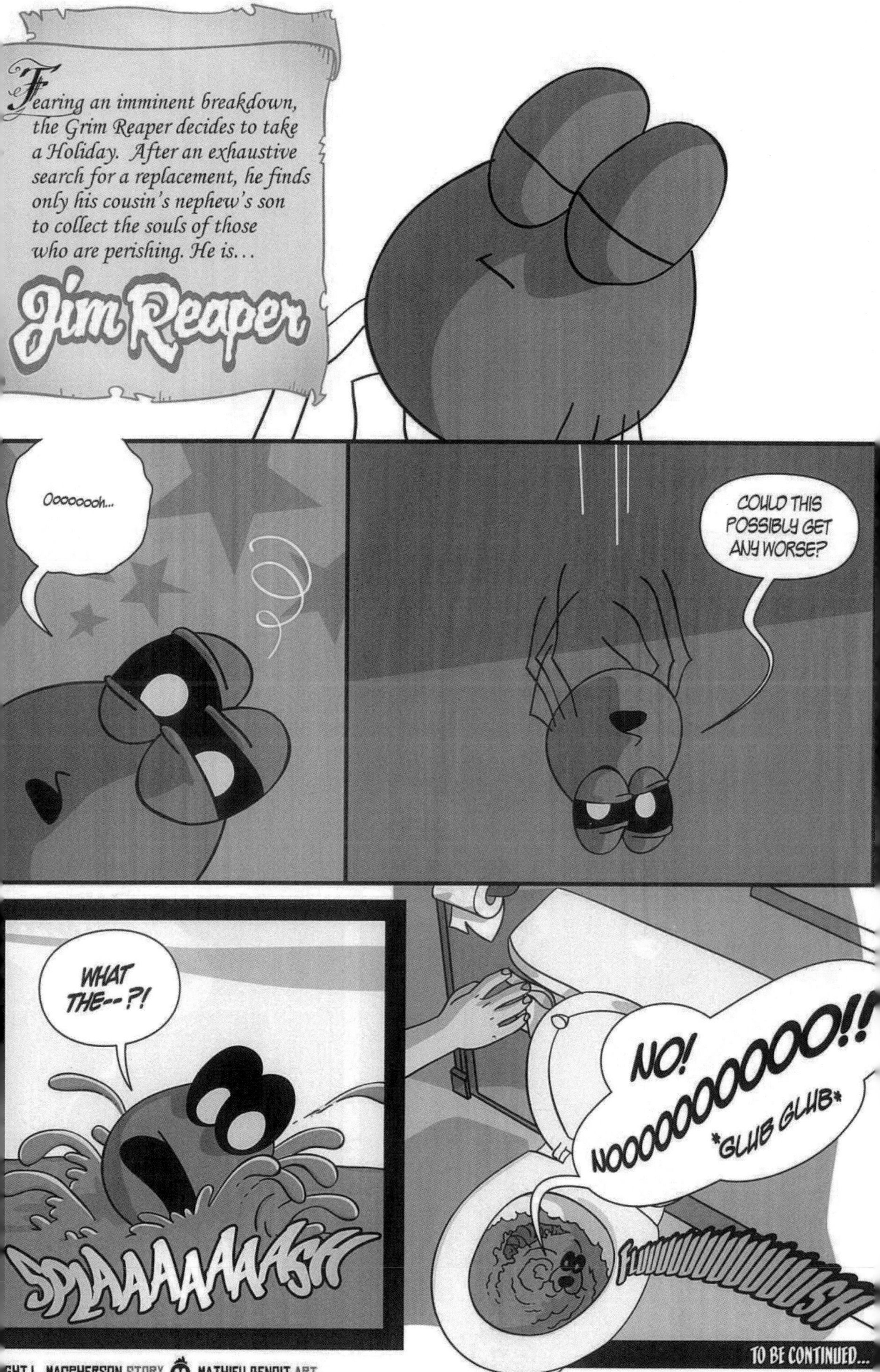
Fearing an imminent breakdown, the Grim Reaper decides to take a Holiday. After an exhaustive search for a replacement, he finds only his cousin's nephew's son to collect the souls of those who are perishing. He is...
Jim Reaper
Ooooooh...
COULD THIS POSSIBLY GET ANY WORSE?
WHAT THE--?!
SPLAAAAAAASH
NO! NOOOOOOOOOOO!!
GLUB GLUB
TO BE CONTINUED...

GHT L. MACPHERSON STORY MATHIEU BENOIT ART

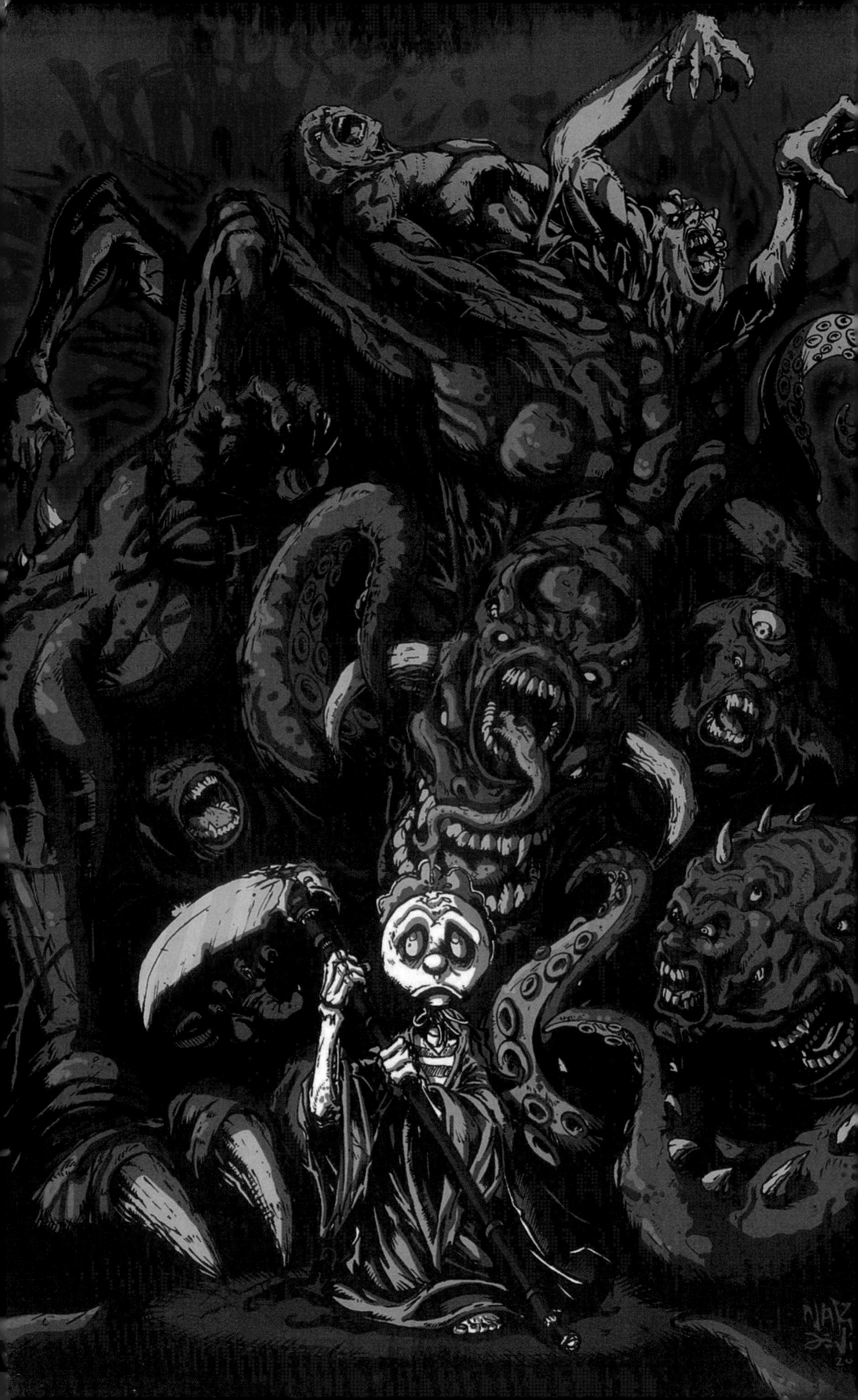

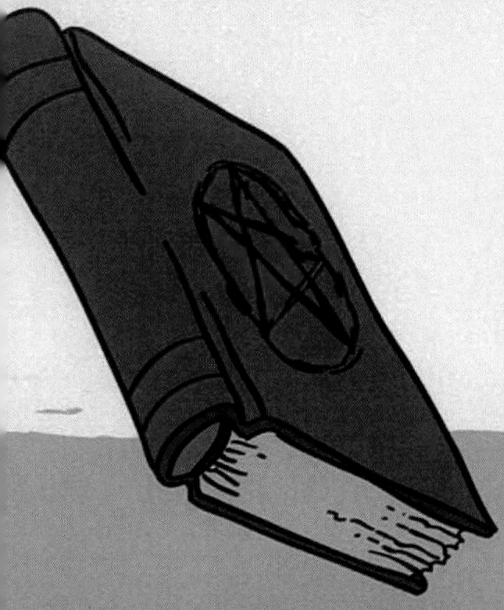

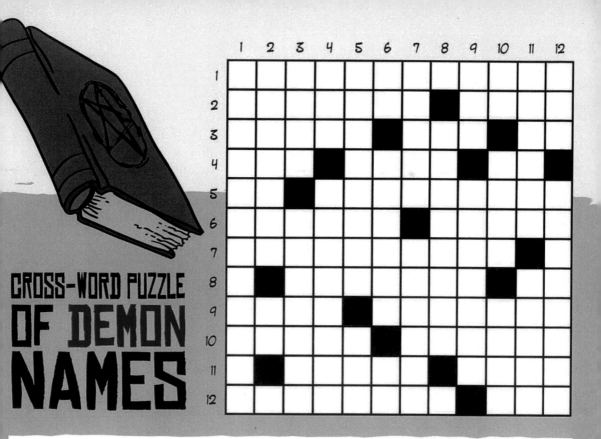

CROSS-WORD PUZZLE OF DEMON NAMES

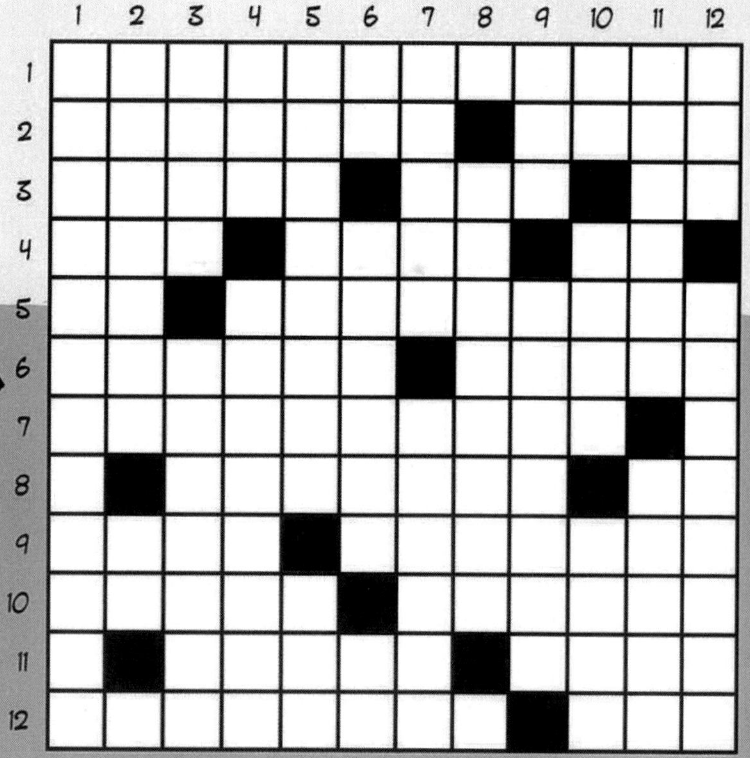

ACROSS

1. This lower-demon made a name for himself by convincing Stephen Hawking that there is no God.
2. This demon won the All-Demon League Bowling Championship in 1456 BC.
3. This demon made a sculpture of Satan using only refried beans.
4. This demon soldier attempted to over-throw Satan in 35 AD.
5. This lower-demon discovered how many licks it takes to get to the center of a Tootsie-Roll pop.
6. This demon attemped to displace Satan as the All-Hell breakdancing champion in 1980.
7. This is another name for the demon philosopher Vxqerdop's Book "Hell Sucks": "_____________."
8. "Ex zyter ________________!!" This is what Satan says about his rule in Hell.
9. Who was the famous husband of Queen Xzyterte?
10. This demon created the Rubik's Cube.
11. Who won the All-Hell arm-wrestling Championship in 1236 BC, displacing undefeated Byqwyer the soul-swallower?
12. This demon singer helped Celine Dion pen "My Heart Will Go On."

DOWN [OUR FAVORITE]

1. What demon holiday was founded by Yiertbycasel in 66 AD?
2. What famous road in the Center Ring District features the legendary Xxa Ehtdat Tavern?
3. This demon convinces people who cannot sing to audition for American Idol.
4. "___ _______________!!" This was the rallying cry of General Bvvxnreyghaw at the Battle of the Great Fall.
5. This demon won the pie eating competition in 1908 AD, despite not having a mouth.
6. This popular demon is known in the mortal world as "Criss Angel."
7. When captured by an angel, this demon cried like a little sissy girl. We have pictures to prove it.
8. "__ _______________ " means "More tacos, please" in demon tongue.
9. This legendary demon helped create the television show "Full House," for which he was severely punished, I might add.
10. In 442 BC, this demon won the All-Hell Hopscotch Championship at the age of 666.
11. This cross-gender demon tricked Beelzebub into having sex with him/her--TWICE. HAHAHAHA. Oh wait-- he's watching.
12. This demon broke the record for longest tango by defeating Mnewfsqaxzpo the Not-so-Grand in 918 BC.

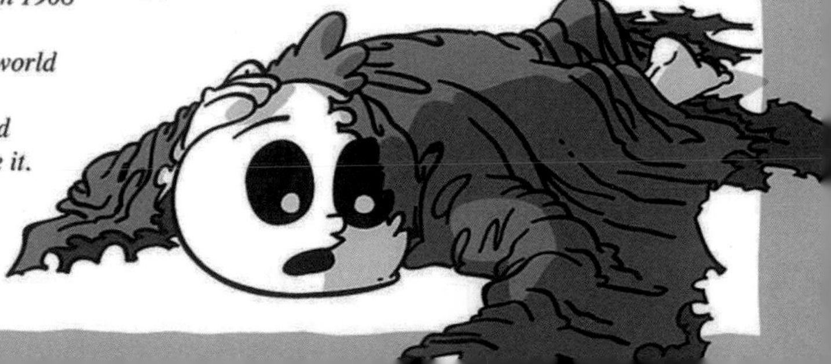

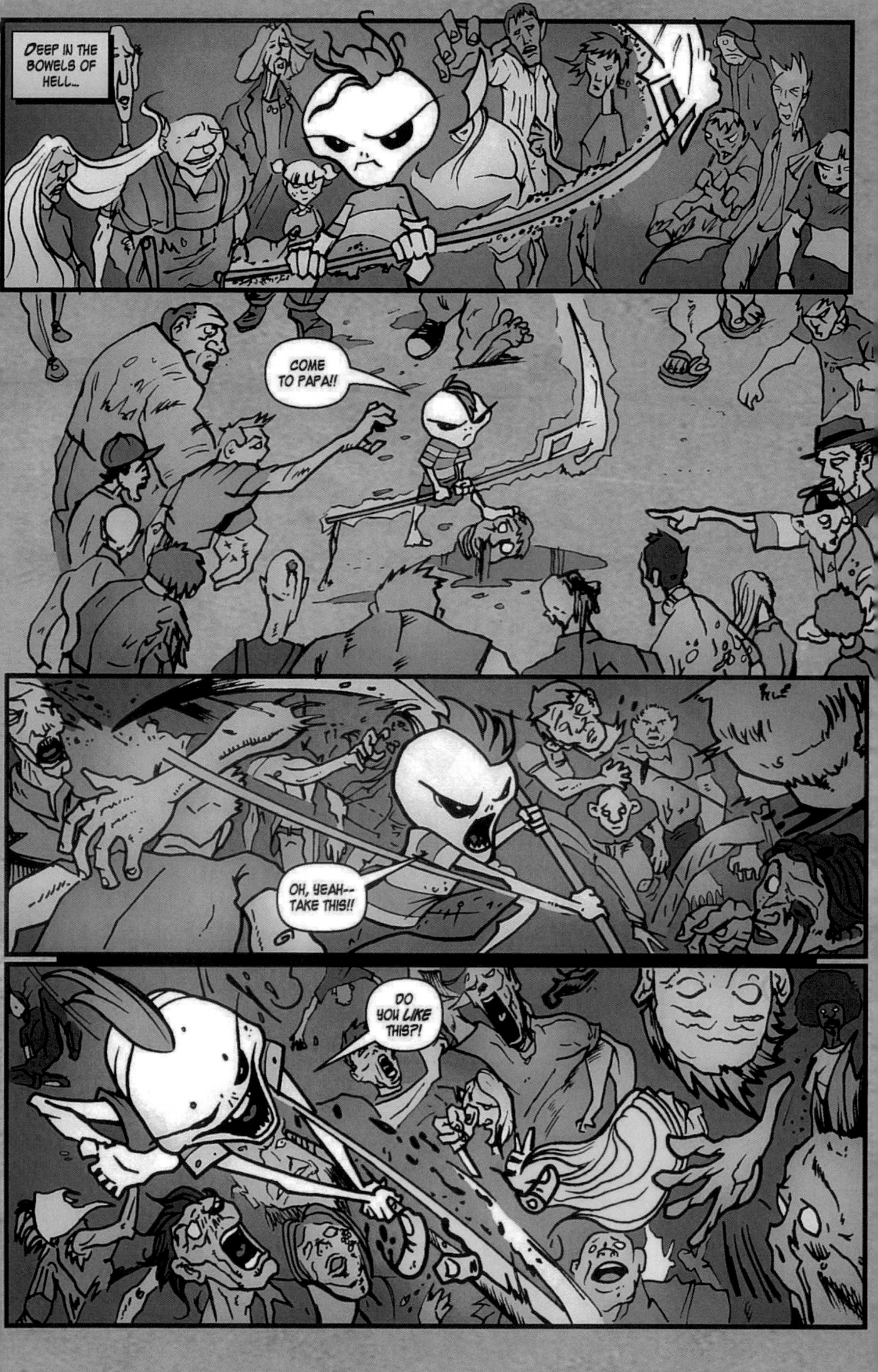
DEEP IN THE BOWELS OF HELL...
COME TO PAPA!!
OH, YEAH-- TAKE THIS!!
DO YOU LIKE THIS?!

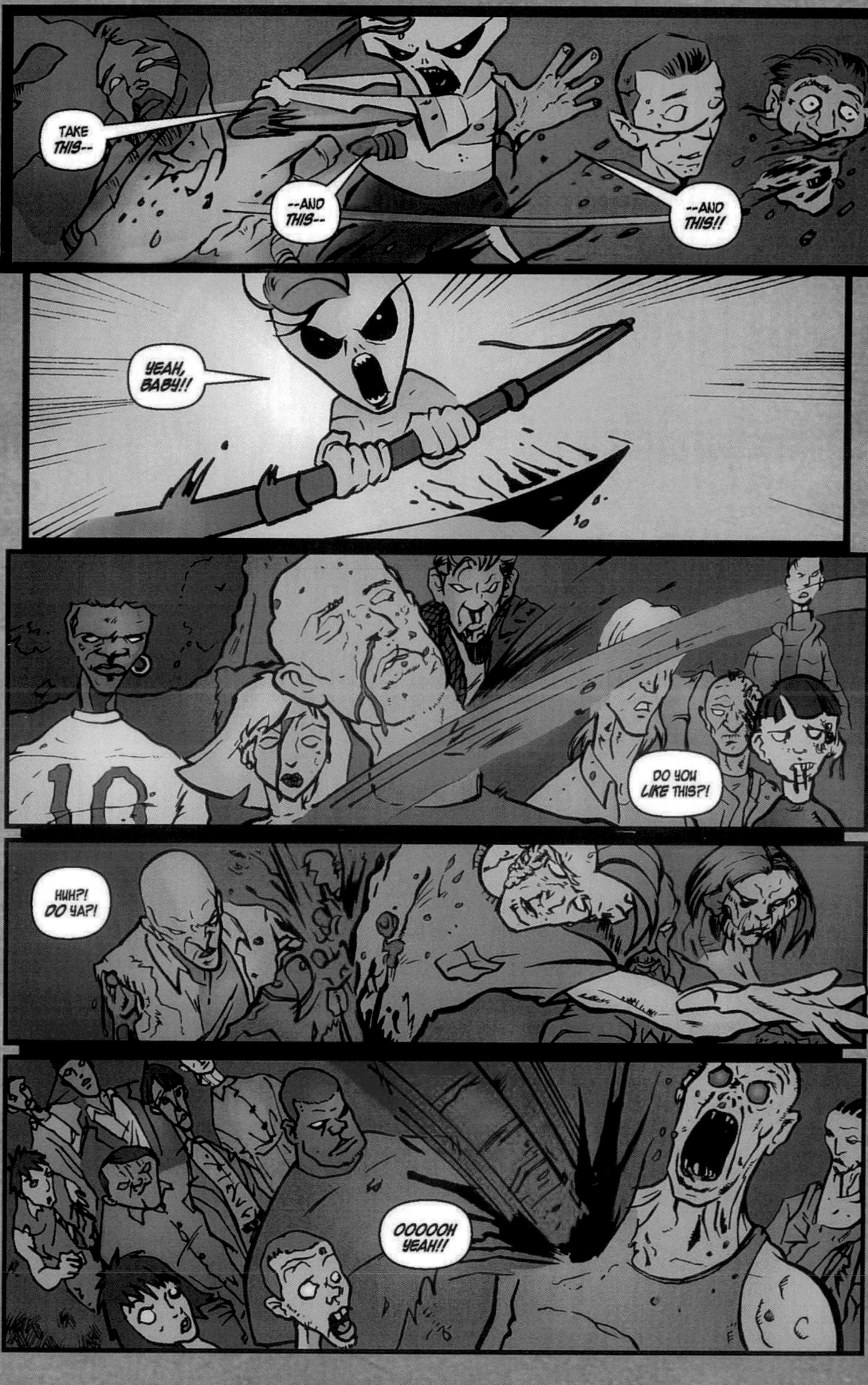
TAKE THIS--
--AND THIS--
--AND THIS!!
YEAH, BABY!!
DO YOU LIKE THIS?!
HUH?! DO YA?!
OOOOOH YEAH!!

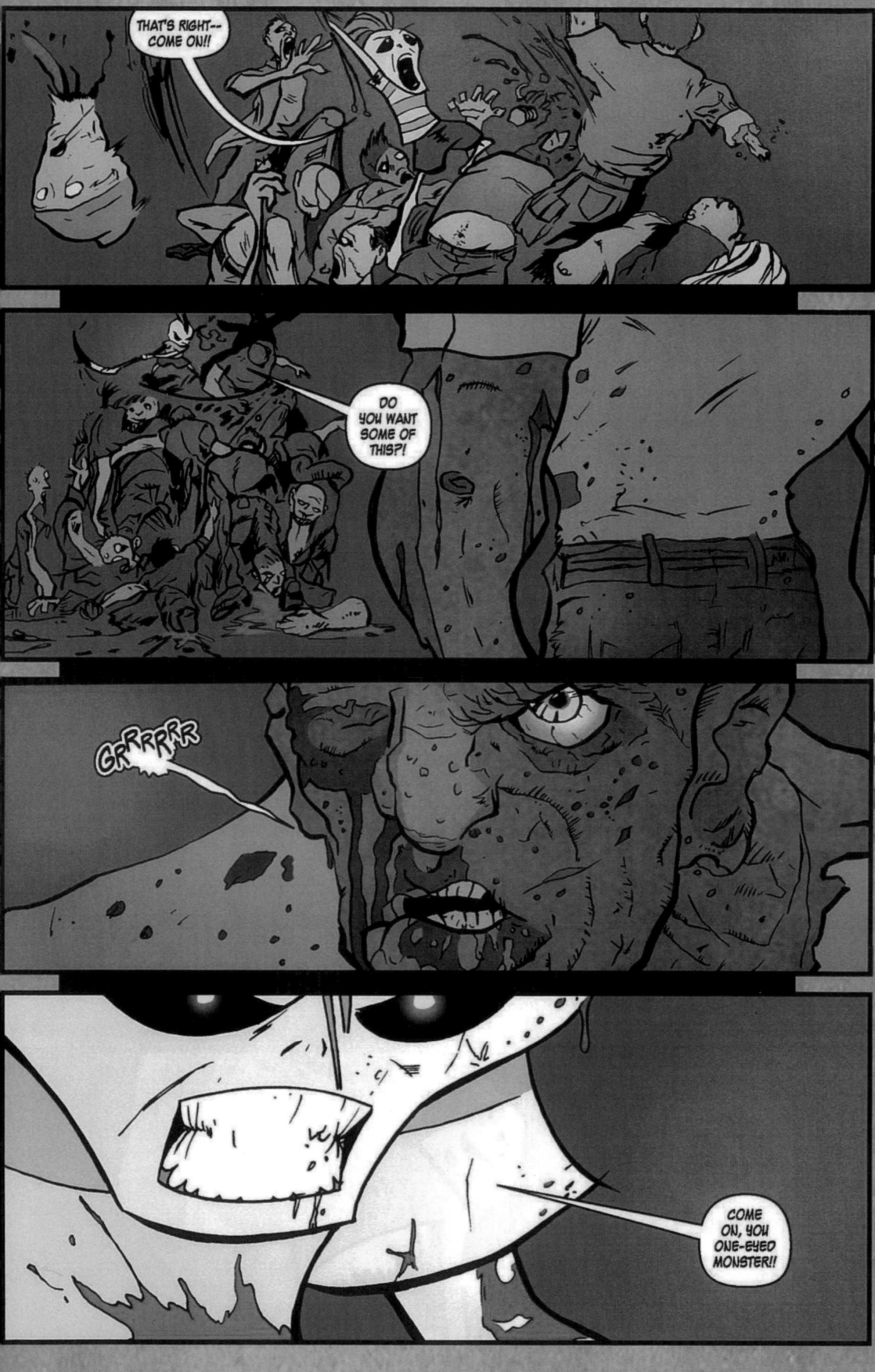
THAT'S RIGHT--
COME ON!!
DO YOU WANT SOME OF THIS?!
GRRRRRR
COME ON, YOU ONE-EYED MONSTER!!

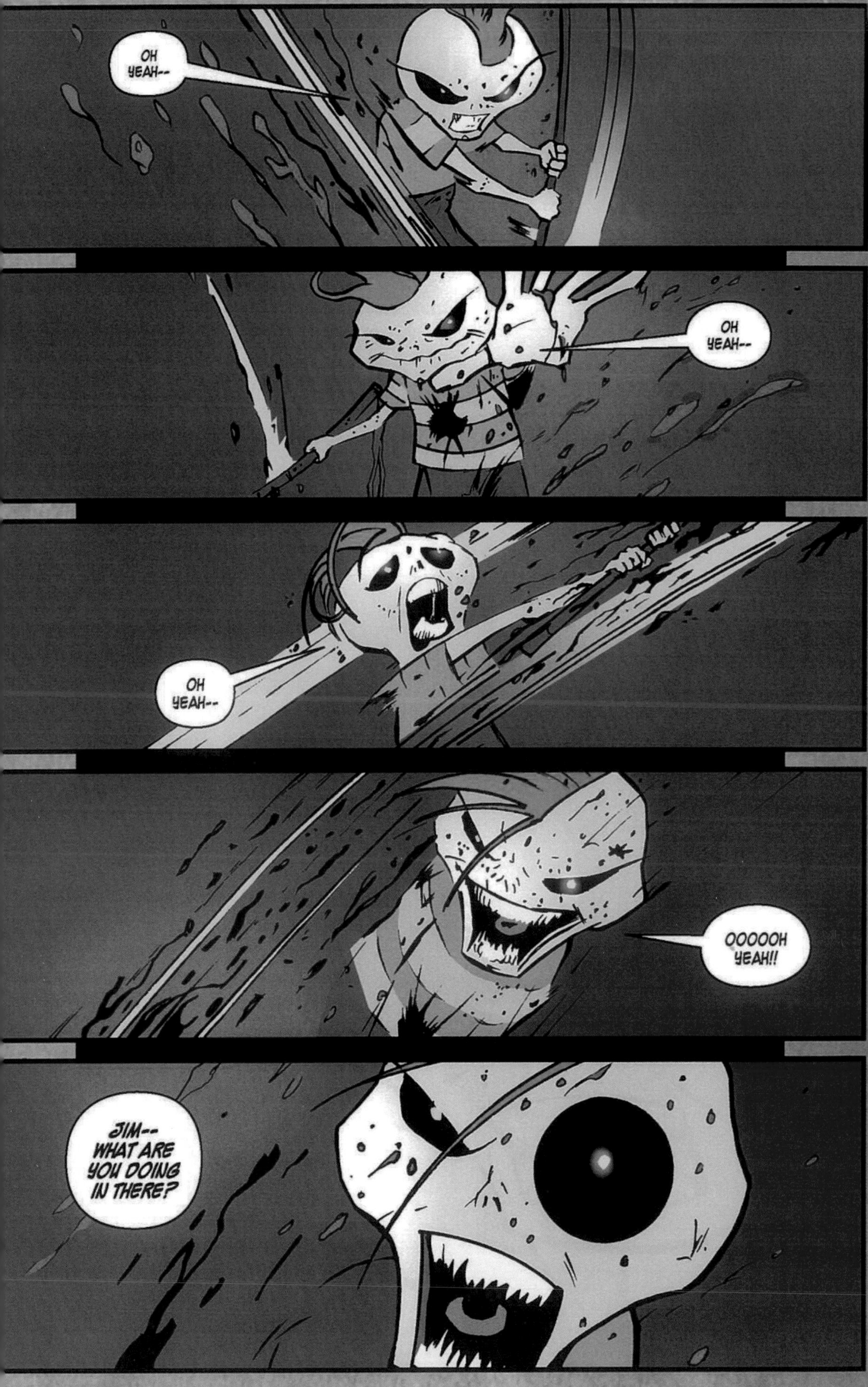
OH YEAH--
OH YEAH--
OH YEAH--
OOOOOH YEAH!!
JIM-- WHAT ARE YOU DOING IN THERE?

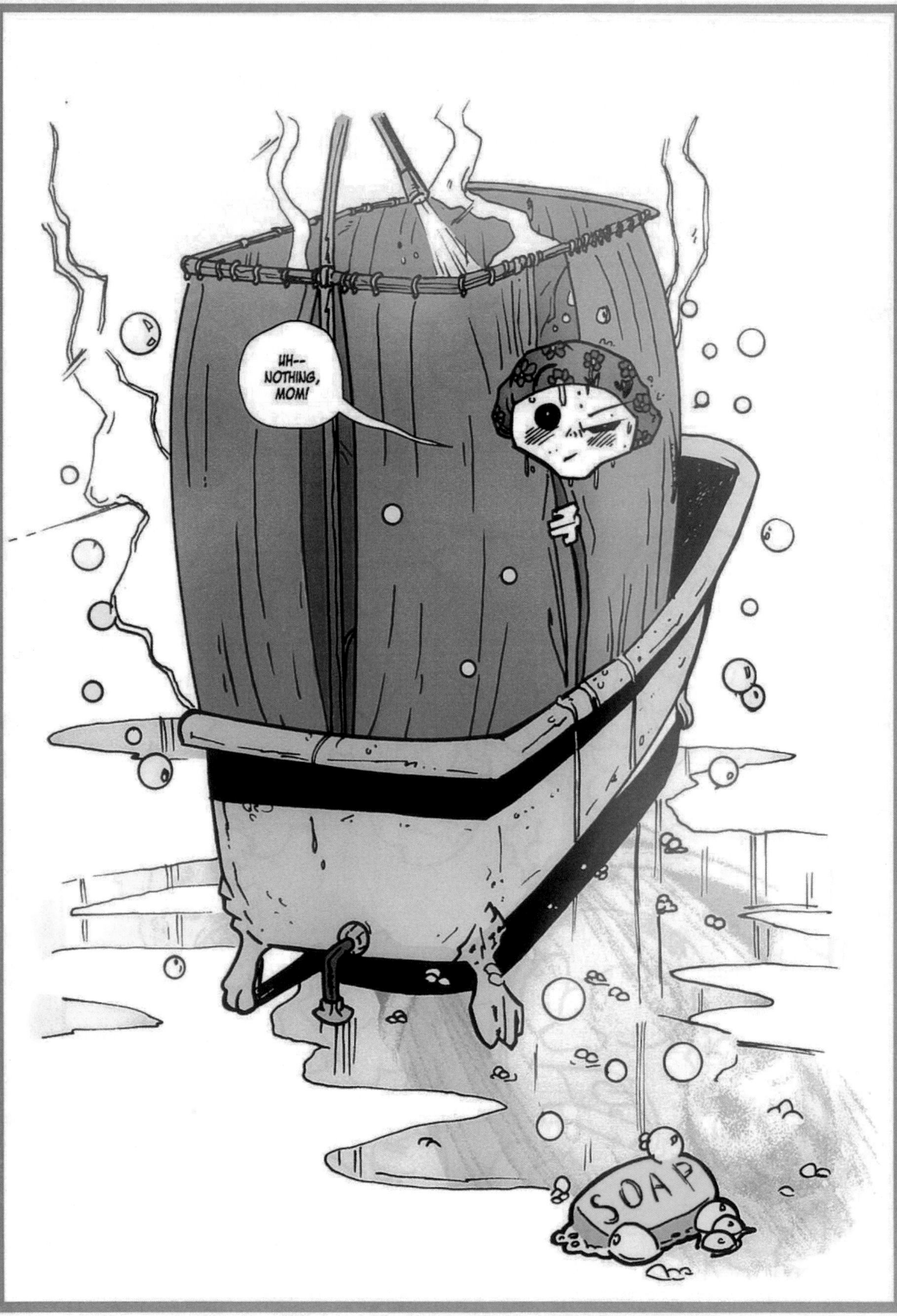
UH--
NOTHING,
MOM!
SOAP

KUNG FU JACK

WRITTEN BY WHOOPY THE WONDER LLAMA
ART BY JORZAC
COLORS BY MICHAEL WULF
LETTERS BY THOMAS MAUER

COLOR THE DAMNED

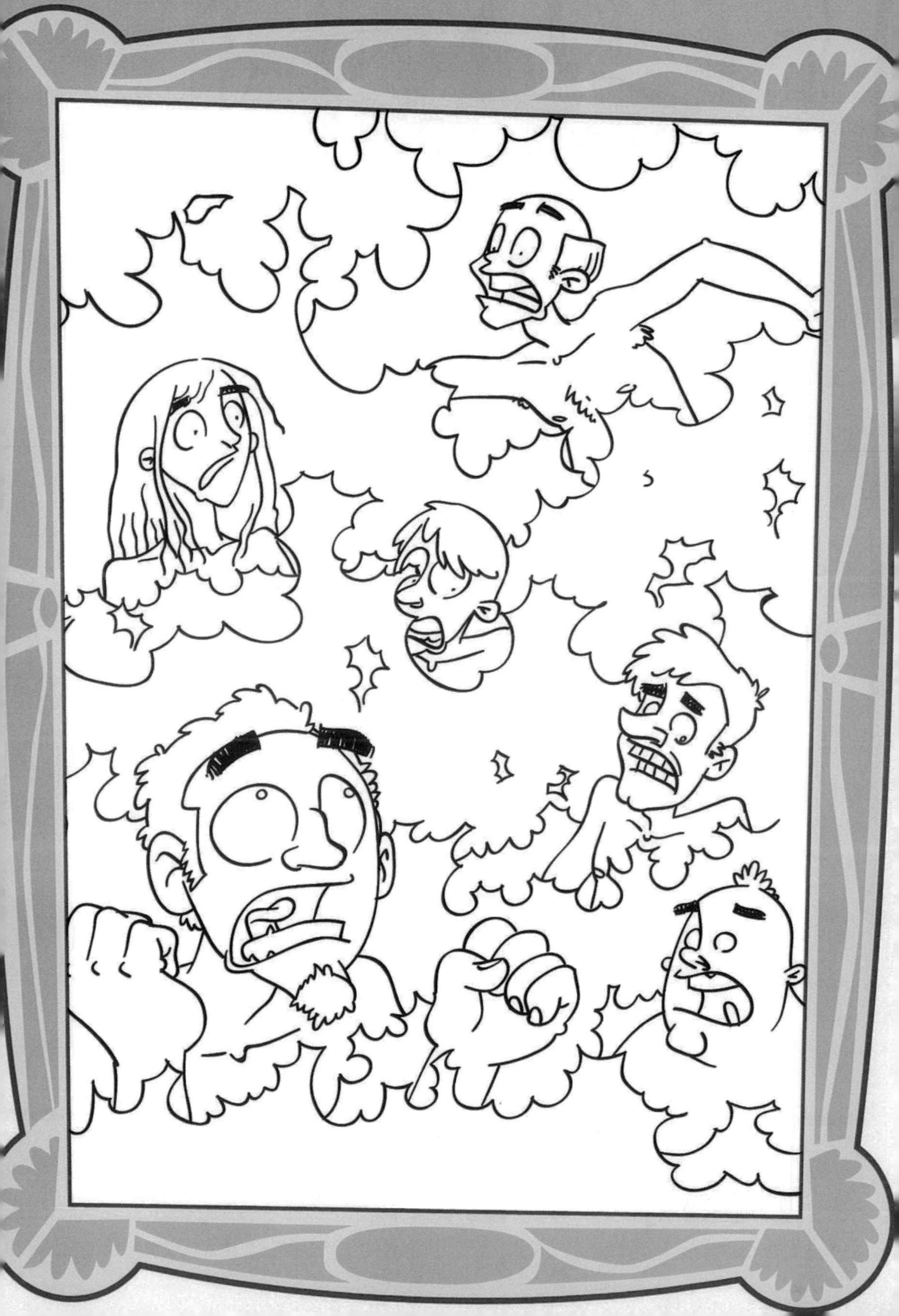

HELP JIM FIND HIS WAY TO HELL

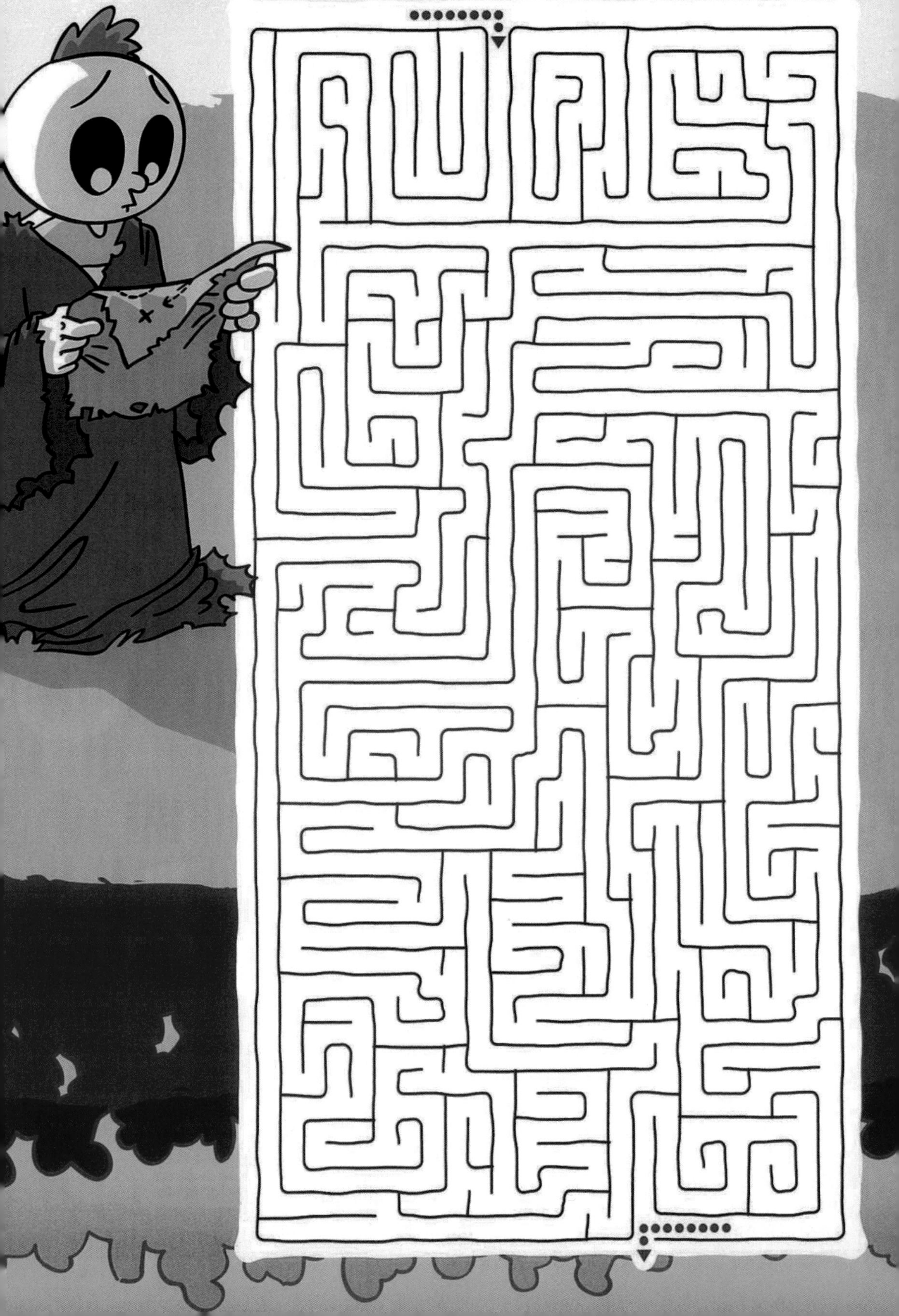

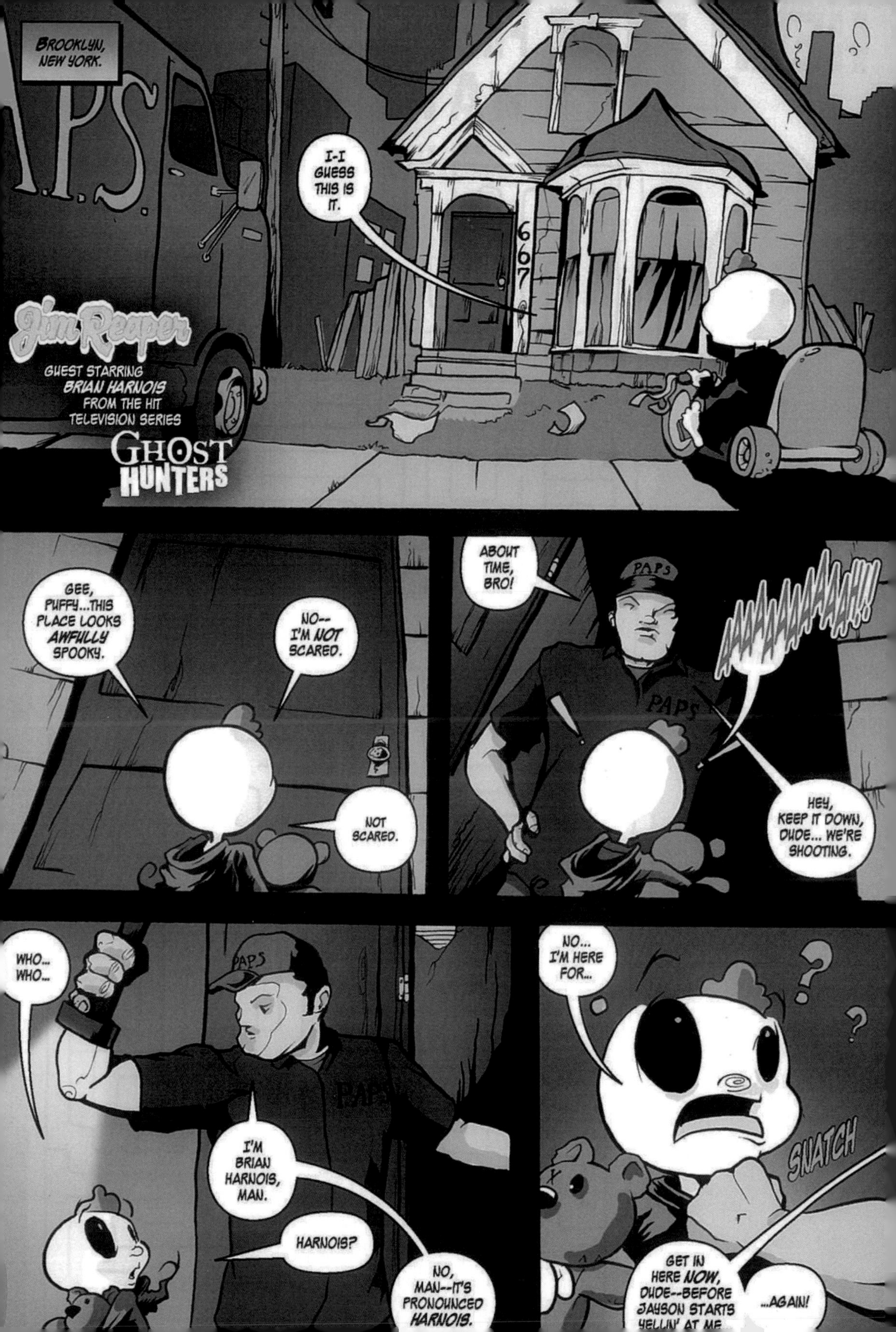
BROOKLYN, NEW YORK.
I-I GUESS THIS IS IT.
Jim Reaper
GUEST STARRING BRIAN HARNOIS FROM THE HIT TELEVISION SERIES
GHOST HUNTERS
GEE, PUFFY...THIS PLACE LOOKS AWFULLY SPOOKY.
NO-- I'M NOT SCARED.
NOT SCARED.
ABOUT TIME, BRO!
AAAAAAAAAAAH!!
HEY, KEEP IT DOWN, DUDE... WE'RE SHOOTING.
WHO... WHO...
I'M BRIAN HARNOIS, MAN.
HARNOIS?
NO, MAN--IT'S PRONOUNCED HARNOIS.
NO... I'M HERE FOR...
SNATCH
GET IN HERE NOW, DUDE--BEFORE JAYSON STARTS YELLIN' AT ME...
...AGAIN!

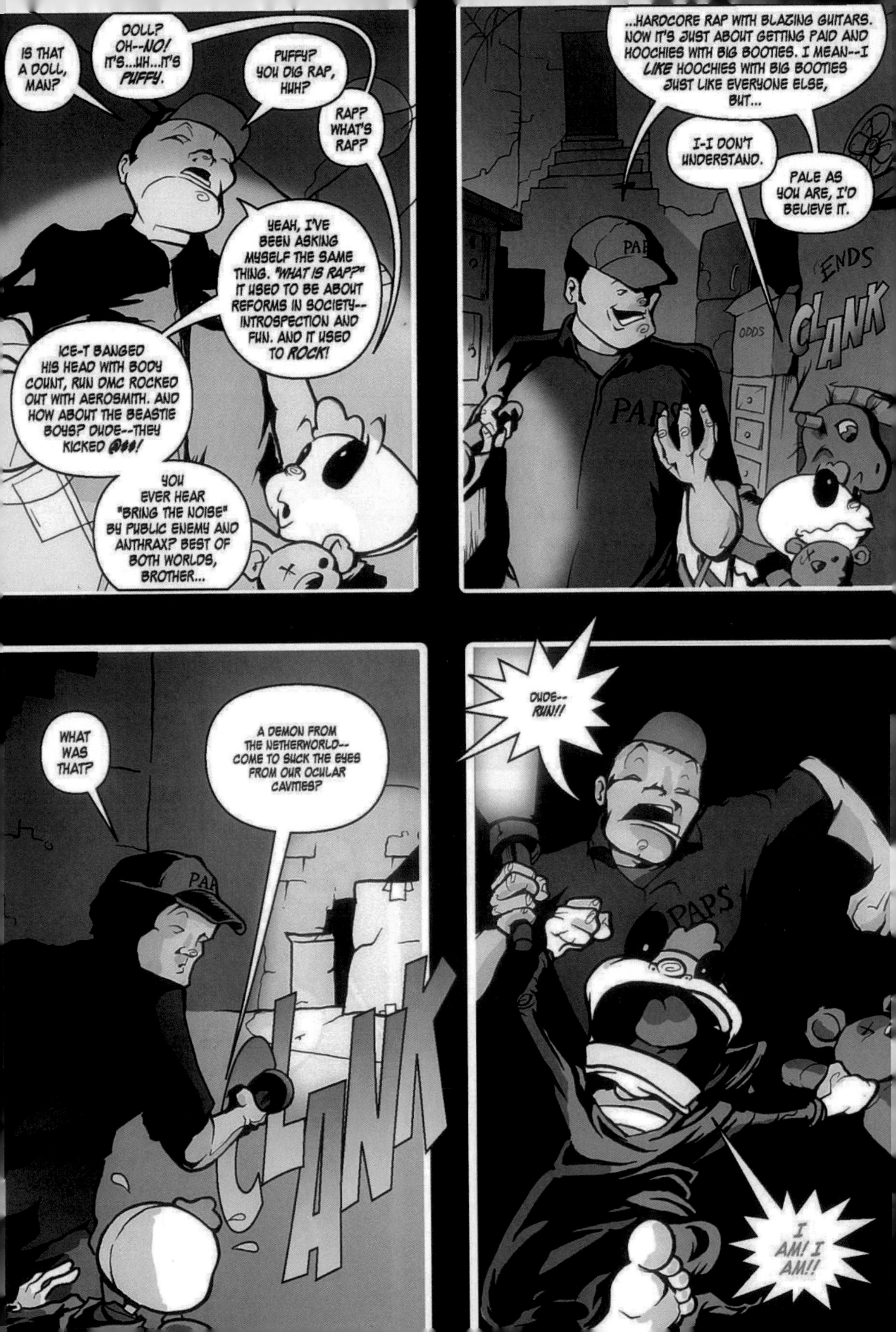

IS THAT A DOLL, MAN?
DOLL? OH--NO! IT'S...UH...IT'S PUFFY.
PUFFY? YOU DIG RAP, HUH?
RAP? WHAT'S RAP?
YEAH, I'VE BEEN ASKING MYSELF THE SAME THING. "WHAT IS RAP?" IT USED TO BE ABOUT REFORMS IN SOCIETY-- INTROSPECTION AND FUN. AND IT USED TO ROCK!
ICE-T BANGED HIS HEAD WITH BODY COUNT, RUN DMC ROCKED OUT WITH AEROSMITH. AND HOW ABOUT THE BEASTIE BOYS? DUDE--THEY KICKED @$$!
YOU EVER HEAR "BRING THE NOISE" BY PUBLIC ENEMY AND ANTHRAX? BEST OF BOTH WORLDS, BROTHER...
...HARDCORE RAP WITH BLAZING GUITARS. NOW IT'S JUST ABOUT GETTING PAID AND HOOCHIES WITH BIG BOOTIES. I MEAN--I LIKE HOOCHIES WITH BIG BOOTIES JUST LIKE EVERYONE ELSE, BUT...
I-I DON'T UNDERSTAND.
PALE AS YOU ARE, I'D BELIEVE IT.
ENDS
ODDS
CLANK
PAPS
WHAT WAS THAT?
A DEMON FROM THE NETHERWORLD-- COME TO SUCK THE EYES FROM OUR OCULAR CAVITIES?
CLANK
DUDE-- RUN!!
I AM! I AM!!

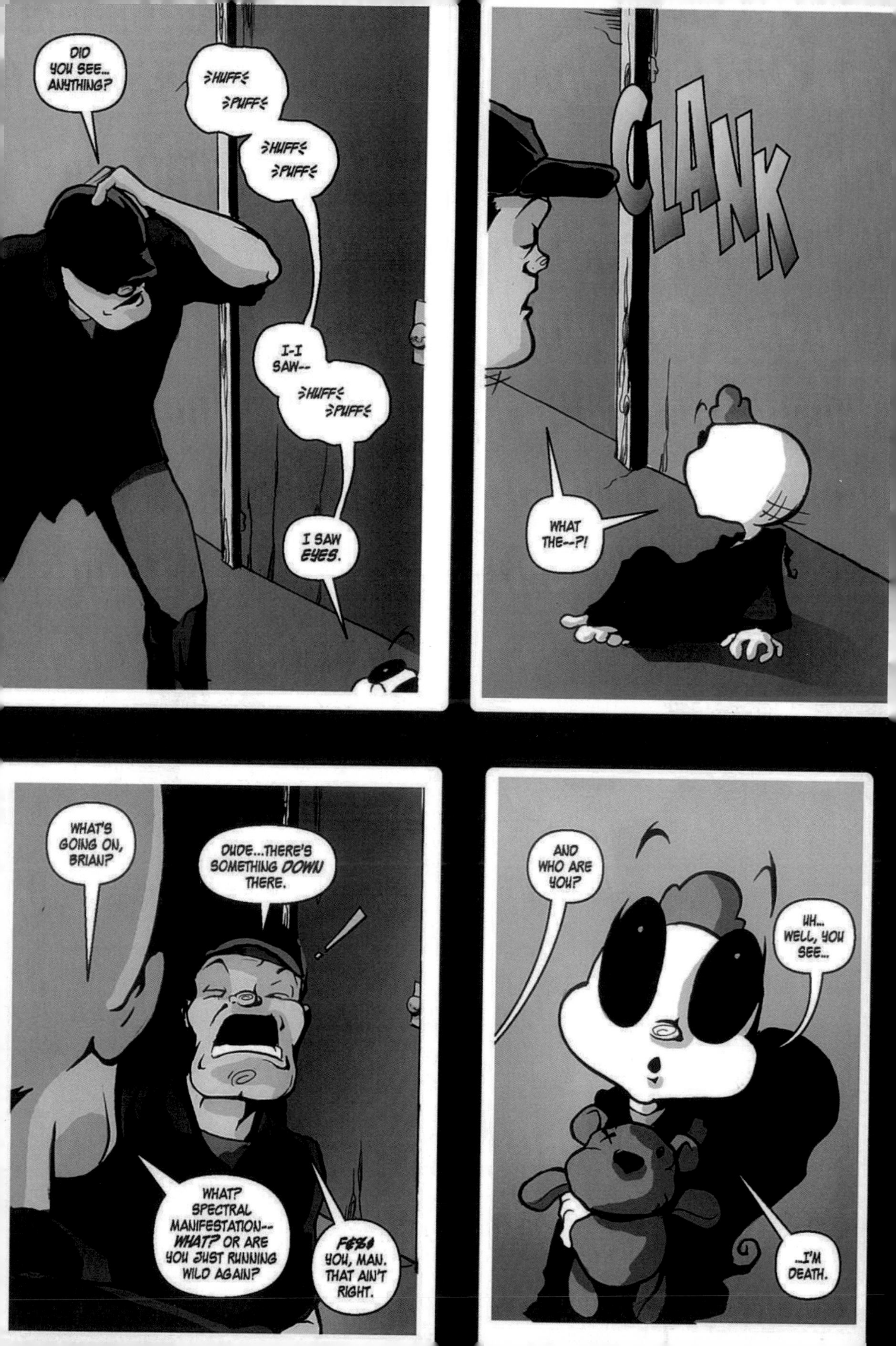

DID YOU SEE... ANYTHING?
≶HUFF≶ ≶PUFF≶
≶HUFF≶ ≶PUFF≶
I-I SAW--
≶HUFF≶ ≶PUFF≶
I SAW EYES.
CLANK
WHAT THE--?!
WHAT'S GOING ON, BRIAN?
DUDE...THERE'S SOMETHING DOWN THERE.
!
WHAT? SPECTRAL MANIFESTATION-- WHAT? OR ARE YOU JUST RUNNING WILD AGAIN?
F&%$ YOU, MAN. THAT AIN'T RIGHT.
AND WHO ARE YOU?
UH... WELL, YOU SEE...
...I'M DEATH.

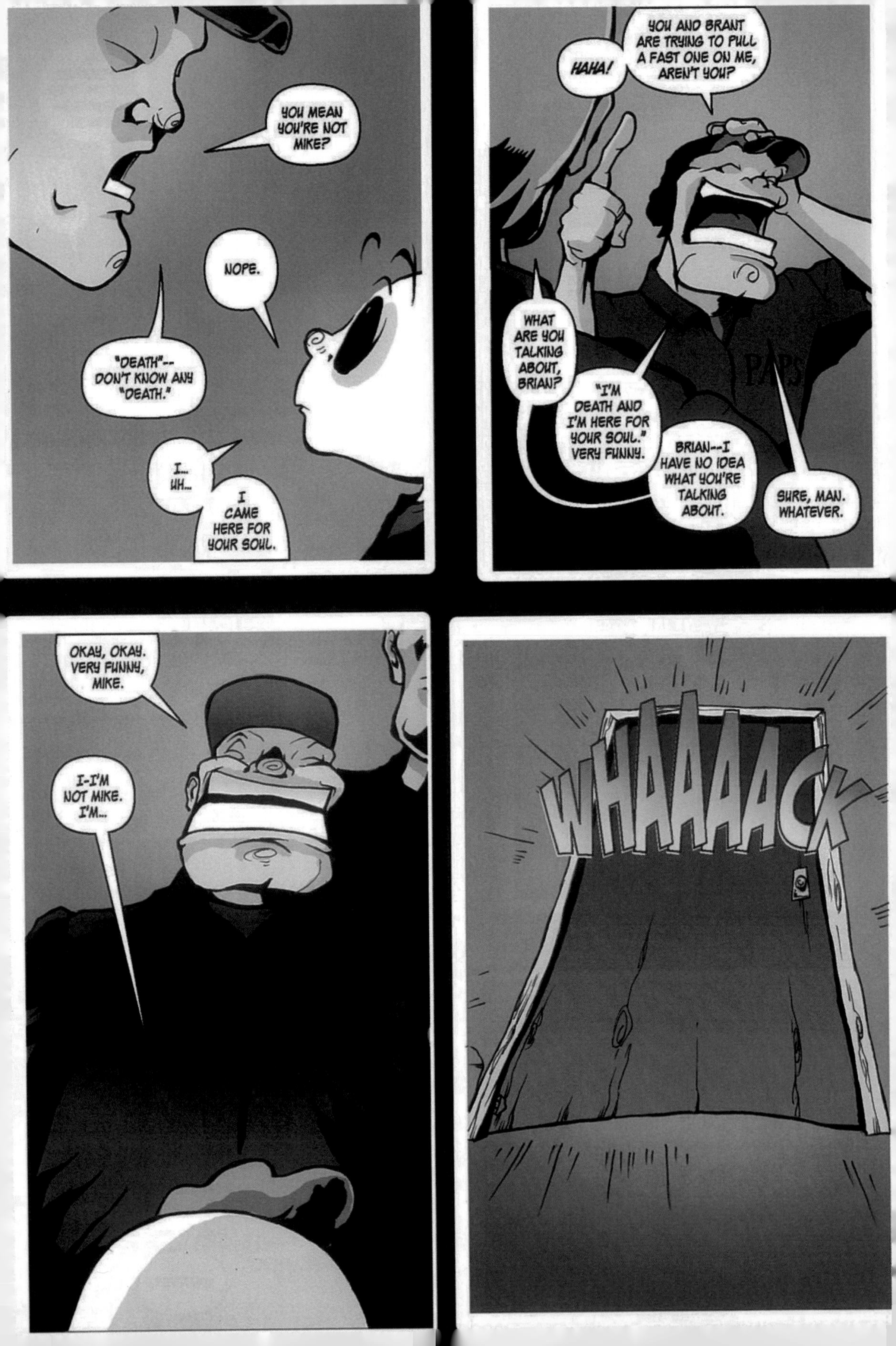
YOU MEAN YOU'RE NOT MIKE?
NOPE.
"DEATH"-- DON'T KNOW ANY "DEATH."
I... UH...
I CAME HERE FOR YOUR SOUL.
HAHA!
YOU AND BRANT ARE TRYING TO PULL A FAST ONE ON ME, AREN'T YOU?
WHAT ARE YOU TALKING ABOUT, BRIAN?
"I'M DEATH AND I'M HERE FOR YOUR SOUL." VERY FUNNY.
BRIAN--I HAVE NO IDEA WHAT YOU'RE TALKING ABOUT.
SURE, MAN. WHATEVER.
PAPS
OKAY, OKAY. VERY FUNNY, MIKE.
I-I'M NOT MIKE. I'M...
WHAAAACK

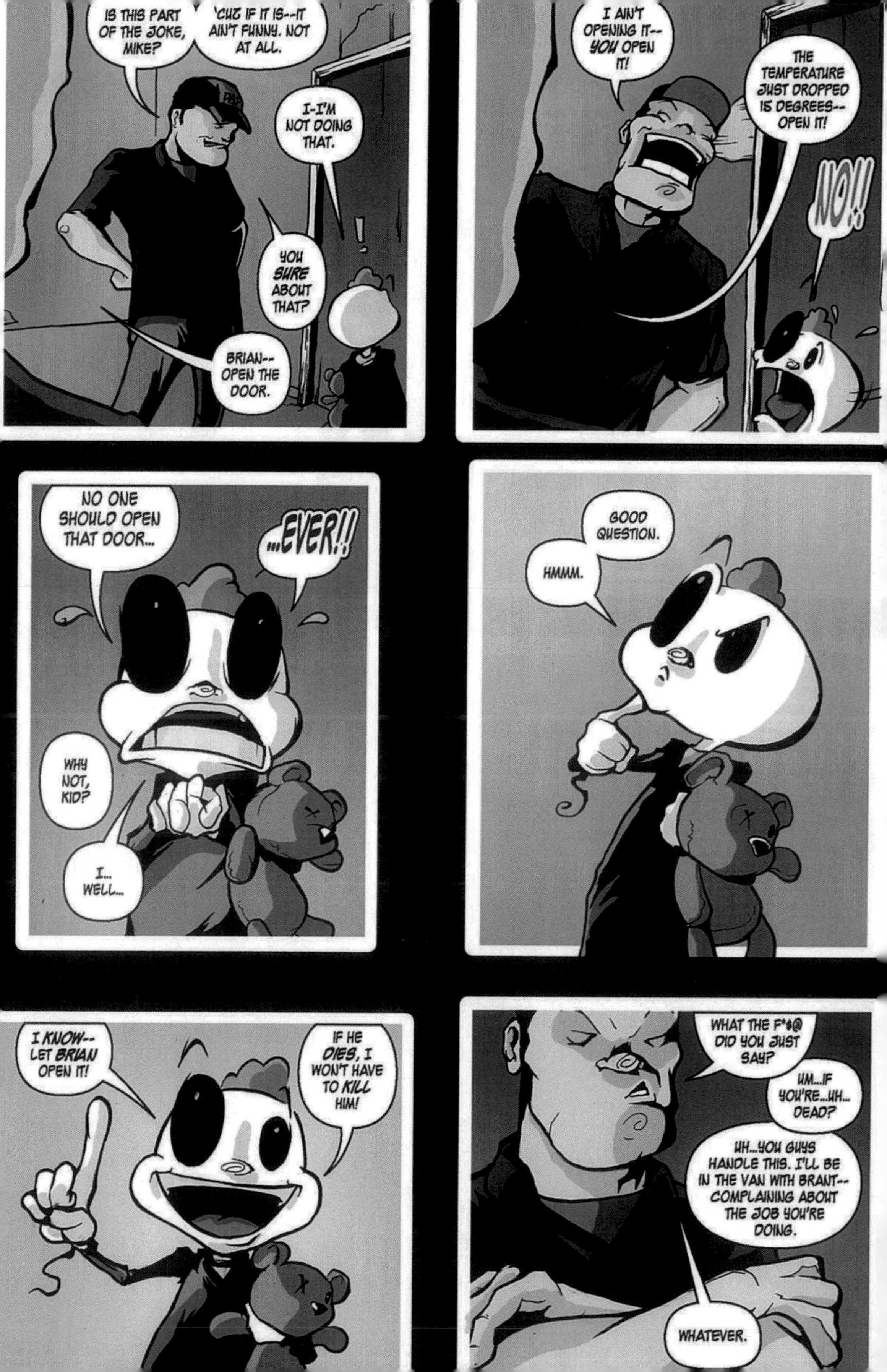
IS THIS PART OF THE JOKE, MIKE?
'CUZ IF IT IS--IT AIN'T FUNNY. NOT AT ALL.
I-I'M NOT DOING THAT.
YOU SURE ABOUT THAT?
BRIAN-- OPEN THE DOOR.
!
I AIN'T OPENING IT-- YOU OPEN IT!
THE TEMPERATURE JUST DROPPED 15 DEGREES-- OPEN IT!
NO!!
NO ONE SHOULD OPEN THAT DOOR...
...EVER!!
WHY NOT, KID?
I... WELL...
GOOD QUESTION.
HMMM.
I KNOW-- LET BRIAN OPEN IT!
IF HE DIES, I WON'T HAVE TO KILL HIM!
WHAT THE F*$@ DID YOU JUST SAY?
UM...IF YOU'RE...UH... DEAD?
UH...YOU GUYS HANDLE THIS. I'LL BE IN THE VAN WITH BRANT-- COMPLAINING ABOUT THE JOB YOU'RE DOING.
WHATEVER.

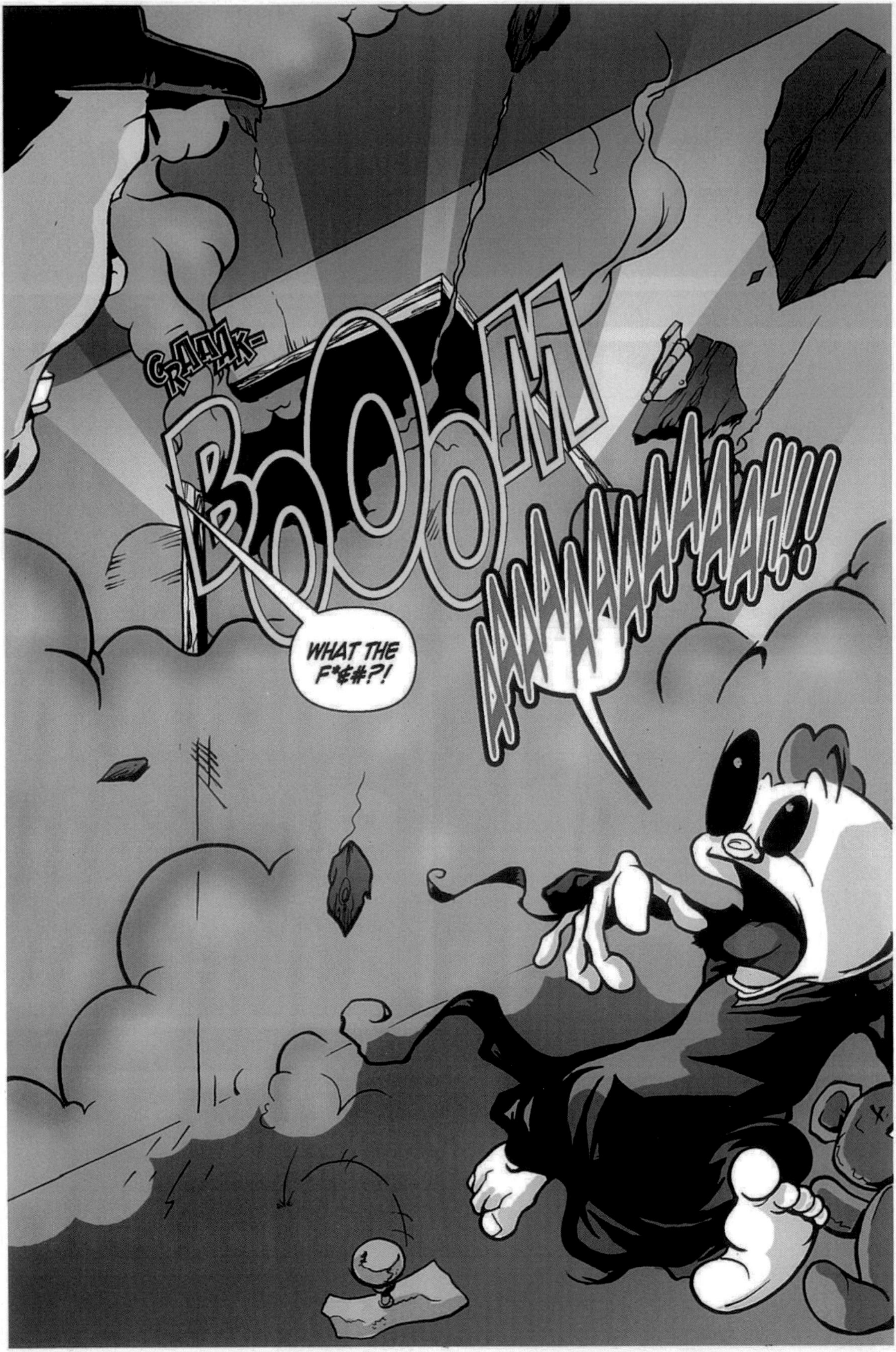
CRAAAK-
BOOOOM
WHAT THE F*$#?!
AAAAAAAAAAAAH!!!

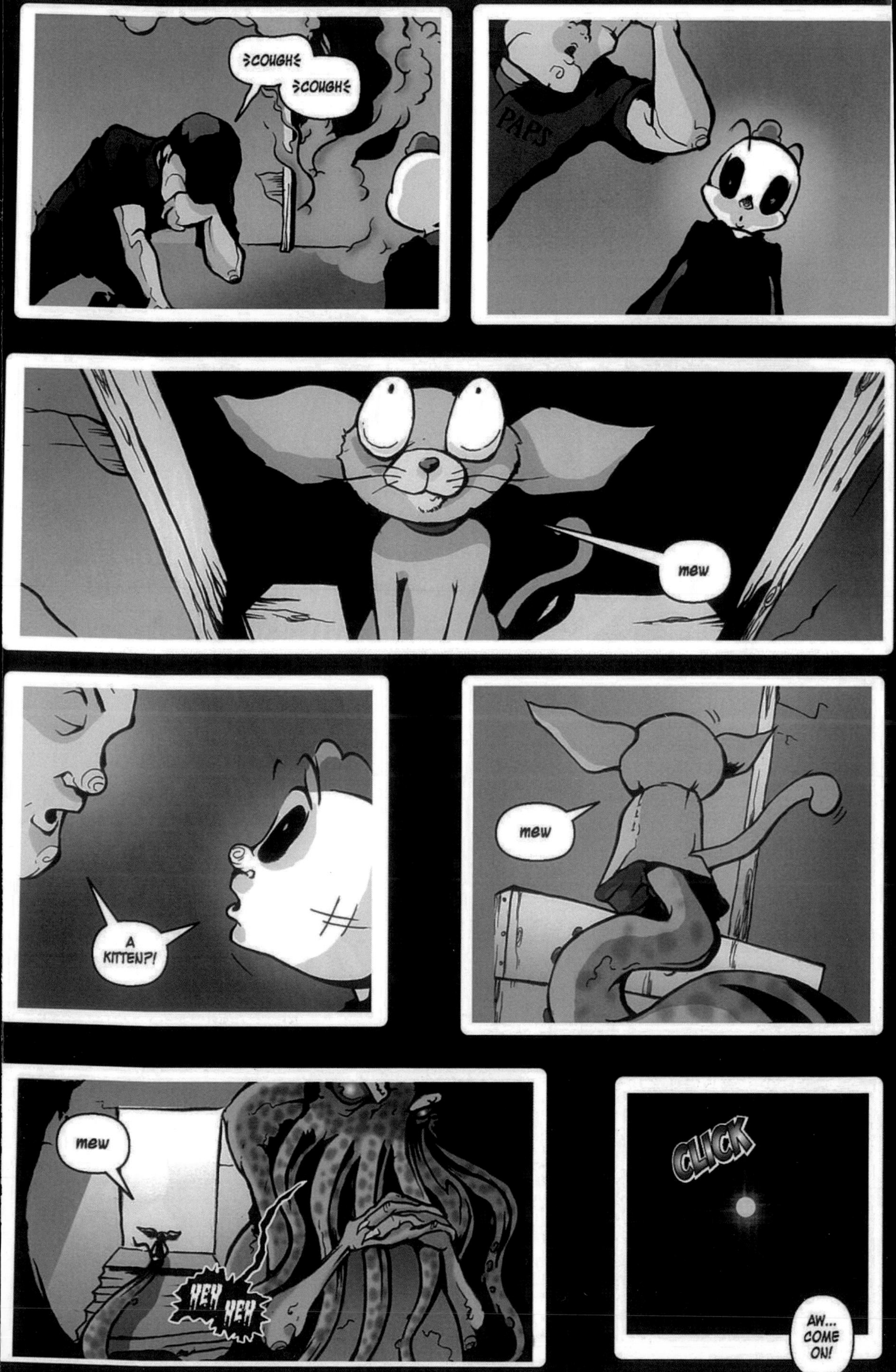
COUGH
COUGH
mew
A KITTEN?!
mew
mew
HEH HEH
CLICK
AW... COME ON!

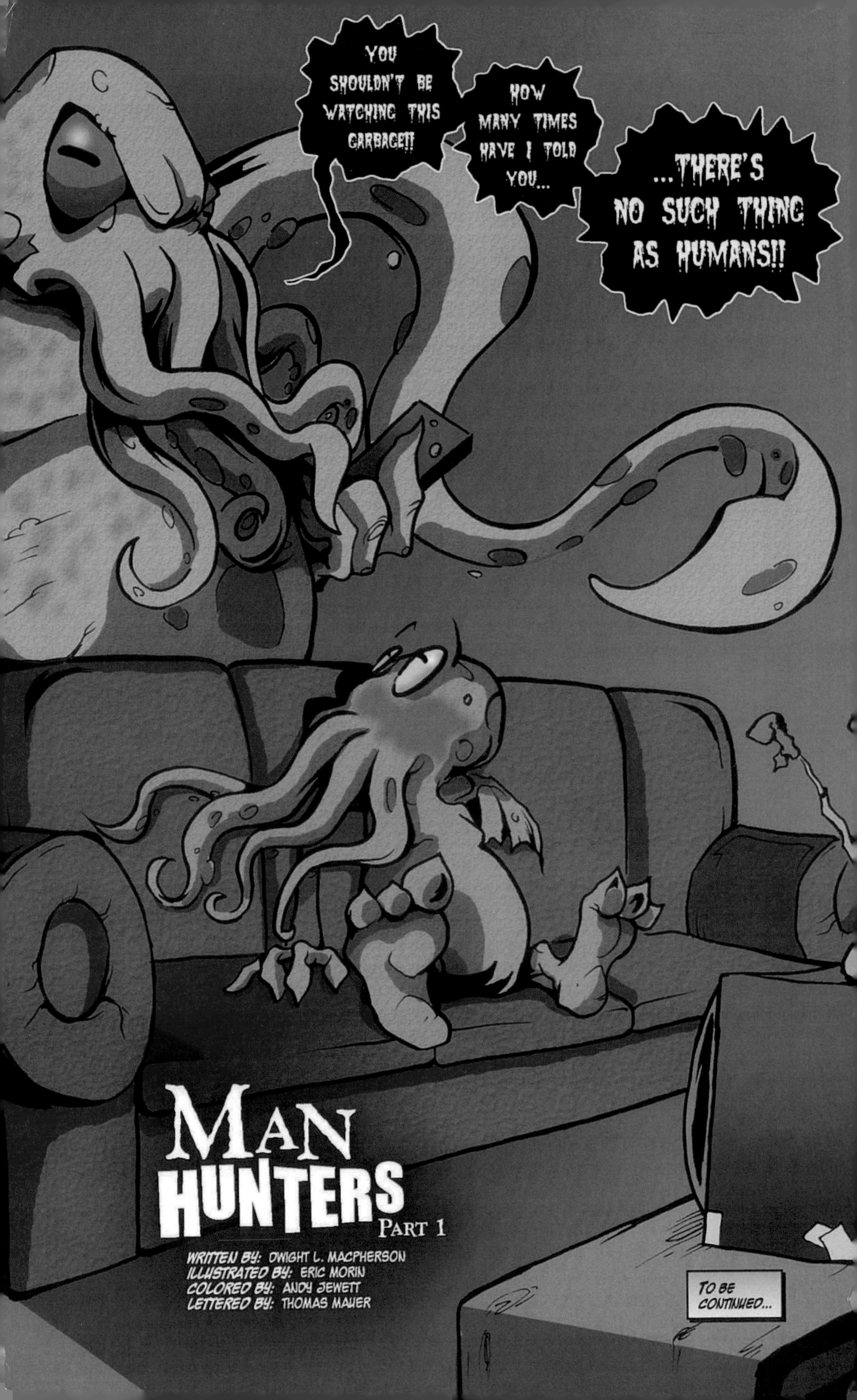
YOU SHOULDN'T BE WATCHING THIS GARBAGE!!
HOW MANY TIMES HAVE I TOLD YOU...
...THERE'S NO SUCH THING AS HUMANS!!
MAN HUNTERS
PART 1
WRITTEN BY: DWIGHT L. MACPHERSON
ILLUSTRATED BY: ERIC MORIN
COLORED BY: ANDY JEWETT
LETTERED BY: THOMAS MAUER
TO BE CONTINUED...